# Kristy and the Missing Fortune

**Other books by
Ann M. Martin**

*Rachel Parker, Kindergarten Show-off*

*Eleven Kids, One Summer*

*Ma and Pa Dracula*

*Yours Turly, Shirley*

*Ten Kids, No Pets*

*Slam Book*

*Just a Summer Romance*

*Missing Since Monday*

*With You and Without You*

*Me and Katie (the Pest)*

*Stage Fright*

*Inside Out*

*Bummer Summer*

BABY-SITTERS LITTLE SISTER series

THE BABY-SITTERS CLUB mysteries

THE BABY-SITTERS CLUB series

# THE BABY-SITTERS CLUB

## Kristy and the Missing Fortune

## Ann M. Martin

AN
**APPLE**
PAPERBACK

SCHOLASTIC INC.
New York Toronto London Auckland Sydney

Cover art by Hodges Soileau

ISBN 0-590-48234-3

Copyright © 1995 by Ann M. Martin. All rights reserved. Published by Scholastic Inc. THE BABY-SITTERS CLUB ® and APPLE PAPERBACKS ® are registered trademarks of Scholastic Inc.

12 11 10 9 8 7 6 5 4 3 2 1          5 6 7 8 9/9 0/0

Printed in the U.S.A.                               40

First Scholastic printing, February 1995

*The author gratefully acknowledges*
*Ellen Miles*
*for her help in*
*preparing this manuscript.*

# CHAPTER 1

"Okay, let's see," I said, thinking out loud. I was sitting at my desk with a notebook open in front of me and a pen in my hand. "If I put Matt at first, maybe Buddy can play left field." I jotted down some notes. "That'll leave third base open for — who?" I paused to think, tapping the pen against my teeth. "Jamie? No, he's too afraid of the ball. He couldn't handle a line drive up the baseline. Nicky? Hmmm . . . maybe!" I wrote down his name.

"Kristy, can I come in?" Karen poked her head into my room.

"Sure," I said, shoving my chair back. "How was school today?"

"Okeydokey," said Karen playfully, giving me a goofy smile as she adjusted her pink-rimmed ·glasses. Karen has blonde hair, blue eyes, and a scattering of freckles. She's seven, and in second grade. Karen is a real live wire, as her father would say. (That means she's full

1

of energy and spunk.) Her father is Watson Brewer, my *step*father. That makes Karen my stepsister. And it's funny: even though we're not related by blood, she and I have a lot in common. For example, I've been called a "live wire" more than once myself.

I'm Kristy Thomas. (Kristin Amanda Thomas, according to my birth certificate.) I'm thirteen and in the eighth grade at Stoneybrook Middle School. I've lived in Stoneybrook — that's Stoneybrook, *Connecticut*, in case you're wondering — all my life. As for looks, I have brown hair and brown eyes, and I'm short for my age. In fact, I'm the shortest person in my class! I'm known for that, and I'm also known for speaking my mind (some people would say "having a big mouth") and for coming up with good ideas. Such as the one for the BSC, or the Baby-sitters Club. I'm president of the BSC, and all my closest friends are members. But more about that later.

"What are you doing?" Karen was asking. She was standing next to me so she could take a peek at my notebook.

"Trying to figure out the Krushers' lineup," I replied.

"Krushers!" Karen said. Her eyes lit up. "Yea! Is it almost time to start practicing?"

"Well . . . not for a while. It's only February, after all. We can't start playing until the snow

2

on the softball field melts. Right?"

"Right," said Karen, looking a little down-cast. "So why are you thinking about it now?"

"Because it's February." I sighed, looking out the window at the cold, gray day. February gets me down, and I guess I'm not the only one. Everybody's kind of in the doldrums during February. Winter's been going on long enough to be boring, and spring is still too far off to seem real. But that day at school, I'd had a conversation that cheered me right up.

It happened at lunchtime. I was sitting in the cafeteria, eating with Mary Anne Spier, my best friend since *forever*, when her steady boyfriend Logan Bruno walked up and plopped down his tray. I was just about to comment on how much his chicken chow mein looked like dog barf (a comment Mary Anne wouldn't have appreciated at all, even though it was true), when Logan said something that totally distracted me.

"Pitchers and catchers report in two weeks!"

"Two *weeks*?" I said. "All *right*!" I made a fist and pumped my arm.

"Report?" asked Mary Anne. "On what? Their activities since the last baseball season? Is that like when our teachers used to make us write those 'What I Did on My Summer Vacation' essays?" She giggled.

Logan and I just stared at her for a second,

3

and then we burst out laughing. Mary Anne's giggles faded abruptly and a hurt look flashed across her face. Right away, I felt terrible for laughing at her. Mary Anne is *extremely* sensitive. Knowing her, I had the feeling she might start crying in another second. Right in the middle of the cafeteria.

I rushed to set her straight. "It's not *report* like a written report," I said. "It's *report* like report for duty. It means they have to show up for spring training in two weeks." I turned to Logan and grinned. "Two *weeks*!" I said. I held up my hand for a high-five and he smacked it.

"That's great," said Mary Anne. "I mean, I *guess* it's great." She paused. "Um, *why* is it great?" she asked tentatively.

This time we were careful not to laugh at her. "Because," explained Logan, "it means spring — and *baseball* — will be here soon."

Logan and I are both *huge* baseball fans. All spring and summer, I live and breathe baseball and softball. A perfect day for me would include *playing*: on a team or just with friends; *coaching*: as you might have guessed, I manage a team called the Krushers; and *watching*: heading for the family room after dinner to check out a Mets game on TV.

That talk with Logan had made me feel much, much better about February. As I rode the bus home after school, I looked out the windows at the dirty, chewed-up snow that partially covered the ground, and instead of feeling depressed, I was able to picture that same ground all green with grass. I imagined the smell of fresh dirt, the feel of a ball smacking into a well-oiled leather glove, the sensation of sliding into third base and beating the throw by a millisecond. Baseball! I could hardly wait. And now it suddenly seemed as if the season were right around the corner.

Which was why I was sitting there at my desk, going over the Krushers lineup. I wanted my team to have its best season ever, and I knew that meant planning, planning, and more planning. The day outside was still cold and gray, but inside my room I could practically feel the sun beating down, the way it does when you're standing at home plate in the middle of July.

"Can I play shortstop this year?" asked Karen. She was still trying to get a glimpse of my notes.

"Shortstop?" I asked.

Karen nodded. "I'm tired of playing in the outfield. Nothing ever happens out there. It's boring!"

Karen had a point. The outfield *can* be boring, especially in the Krushers games. See, most of the kids who play on my team are young. Too young for Little League. And they don't hit the ball very far. Often, as a matter of fact, their biggest hits don't travel much past the pitcher's mound. So I could see why Karen might want to play in the infield: it's the only place to be, if you're interested in action.

The problem is, I have a *lot* of kids to consider. There are about twenty Krushers. I can't play favorites by giving special treatment to family members, especially since Karen isn't the only Krusher who's related to me. Her four-year-old brother Andrew, my step-brother, is on the team, and so is my younger brother David Michael, who's seven.

Just to fill you in on the rest of my family, I also have two *older* brothers, Charlie and Sam. Charlie's seventeen, and has his driver's license. Sam is fifteen. For a long time, our family consisted of me and my mom plus my three brothers. That was because my dad pretty much ran out on us, back when David Michael was a baby. We don't hear from my dad often — I think he lives in California — and we don't talk about him much, either.

Fortunately, my mom happens to be an amazing woman. (She's one of my heroes, and a real role model.) She held our family together for years, and I know it wasn't easy for her to bring up four kids by herself. I did what I could to help, which mainly meant baby-sitting a *lot* for David Michael, but it was still a struggle. Things turned around for us not long ago, though, when my mom met Watson. To be honest, I wasn't nuts about him at first. He was balding, he told stupid jokes, and he took up all my mom's attention. But I've come to like Watson a lot, even though he's *still* balding and *still* tells stupid jokes, the stupidest jokes in the world.

After my mom married Watson, my family moved across town to his house. Why? Well, because our old house, which was next door to Mary Anne's house, was way too small for us. Watson's is plenty big enough. In fact, it's a *mansion*. See, there's one thing I haven't mentioned about Watson. He's mega-rich, a real live millionaire.

Watson doesn't act like one of those rich people on TV, though. He's just a regular person who happens to make tons of money.

Anyway, once he and my mom were married, they decided they'd like to have a child together, one that belonged to both of them. That's when they adopted Emily Michelle. She's two and a half years old, she's Vietnamese, and she's about the most adorable kid you'll ever meet. Get this: lately, her favorite word is "tylis!" Translated, that means "stylish." We say that to her when she's wearing a new outfit, and when she hears the word she repeats it, striking a model's pose, with one hip thrust out and a hand behind her head. It's a riot.

Soon after Emily Michelle arrived, my grandmother Nannie came to live with us, too, just to help out. She's my mother's mother. Nannie probably has more energy than the rest of us put together. She has a neat old car we call the Pink Clinker, and she's always taking off in it for things such as a bowling tournament or a volunteer's award dinner at the hospital. Nannie's cool.

Nannie moved out for a little while recently, but only because of a misunderstanding. As soon as it was cleared up, she moved back in. The misunderstanding came about when Watson had a minor heart attack (minor, but very, very scary) and decided he wanted to spend *less* time on work and more time with his family. Nannie thought that with Watson home being Mr. Mom, she wasn't needed anymore. Since she didn't want to be "in the way," she moved out, but the Thomas-Brewer household nearly fell apart without her!

These days Watson is still spending most of his time at home (he's still running his company, but he's working out of our house instead of at the office), but Nannie knows how much we need — and *want* — her to live with us. I don't think she'll be moving away again anytime soon.

I can't say I've finished explaining about my family until I tell you about our pets. We have a huge (but basically well behaved) puppy named Shannon. She's a Bernese mountain dog, and she was given to us by a human named Shannon Kilbourne, who happens to be a neighbor, a friend, and a BSC member. We named the dog after the person, and it's worked out fine except for the occasional funny misunderstanding.

We also have a cat named Boo-Boo. He's not one of those comforting, soft cats that like to be held and petted, though. He's old and cranky and unpredictable. The other day I was stroking him, and he opened his mouth and chomped down on my hand in mid-purr.

And Karen and Andrew, who live with us every other month, have two goldfish (named Crystal Light the Second and Goldfishie — don't look at *me!*), plus a rat named Emily Junior, and a hermit crab called Bob that travel back and forth with them.

I suppose I should consider myself lucky that I don't have to figure out what position Bob should be playing on the Krushers. It's hard enough trying to decide how to use the three members of my family who *do* play on the team, not to mention the crowd of other kids who show up at Krushers practices, hoping to be superstars.

"We'll see about shortstop," I promised Karen that day in my room. "If you really think you can handle the position, I'll give you a chance there."

"Really?" asked Karen, her eyes wide. "That is *gigundoly* super!" She got this faraway look in her eyes, and I knew she was picturing herself as a star shortstop in the major leagues. Karen has an imagination that won't quit.

Just then, I happened to glance at my watch. "Whoa!" I said. "It's almost time for me to head over to Claud's for the BSC meeting."

"Can I ride with you?" begged Karen.

"Sure," I said. "It's okay with me if Charlie doesn't mind." Charlie drives me to my friend Claudia Kishi's house for BSC meetings. Since I moved across town, it's too far to walk.

Karen ran to find Charlie. I took one last glance at the notes I'd made, and thought one more time about how great it would be to stand on a baseball diamond feeling soft green grass beneath my feet. Then I grabbed my visor and headed downstairs. It was time to forget about the Krushers for the moment, and concentrate on the other important "team" in my life: the BSC.

# CHAPTER 2

During the drive to Claudia's, Karen, Charlie, and I talked about three things: baseball, baseball, and baseball. Charlie was as excited about the coming season as Karen and I were. He and Sam are both huge fans, and they both love to play ball.

"I'm going to go home and oil my glove," he told me, as he stopped the car, which was rattling a little and making a strange coughing noise, in front of Claud's house. (We call Charlie's car the Junk Bucket. Guess why.)

"Good idea," I said. "Maybe I'll do mine later, too. Thanks for the ride! 'Bye, Karen!" I slammed the car door shut — it took two tries — and headed into the Kishis'. Their front door is always unlocked on Monday, Wednesday, and Friday afternoons. Those are the days the BSC meets, and the members are used to letting themselves in.

I took the stairs up to the second floor two

at a time, pretending I was doing wind-sprints at softball practice. By the time I burst into Claud's room, I was a little out of breath. (I'm going to need some spring training myself, I guess.) "Hey!" I said, greeting Claudia, who was the only BSC member in the room so far. I was early, as usual. Our meetings run from five-thirty until six, but I like to arrive by five-twenty or so. Just call me Miss Punctuality.

Claudia, who was sitting cross-legged on her bed, looked up from the scarf she was knitting. She was using three colors of yarn: purple, green, and a peculiar shade of orange. "Hi, Kristy," she said. She held up the scarf. "What do you think?"

"I — um," I began. I didn't want to tell her what I *really* thought. Even old insensitive me knows that honesty is not always the best policy. I decided to make a joke out of it. "You want my expert opinion?" I asked. "It's *dahling*, dahling."

Claud laughed. She knows that I know — and care — absolutely nothing about fashion. My idea of dressing up means wearing a clean, new pair of jeans with my usual turtleneck and running shoes. And I couldn't tell you how to apply blusher, or even what it's for, exactly. The other BSC members are a little more advanced in these areas. Claudia, for one. To tell you the truth, she's a lot more advanced, which will be obvious when I try to explain what she was wearing that day. In fact, I'll describe what each of my friends wore to the meeting, and maybe that'll give you some idea of what they're like. I know the way I dress tells a lot about me, so I guess it works the same way for everyone.

Actually, before I describe my friends, maybe I should explain just a little bit more about what the BSC is and how it works. The club is really a business, which would make me the CEO (chief executive officer — Watson taught me that) and founder. I founded the Baby-sitters Club one day back when I was in seventh grade. My mom was trying like crazy to find a sitter for David Michael (my brothers and I had other plans for the afternoon), and after I'd listened to her make about a dozen phone calls I had a brainstorm. What if I got together with a few other friends who liked to baby-sit, and we let parents know that they could call *one* number and reach a whole group of experienced, responsible, available baby-sitters?

The idea worked like a charm, and the club has been growing and changing ever since. We now have seven members plus two associate members, and plenty of regular clients.

We hardly ever have to advertise anymore. (When we do, we hand out fliers, or take out classified ads.)

The BSC is very well organized. We have a record book, in which we keep track of our schedules, our earnings, and client names and addresses; a club notebook, in which we write up all the jobs we go on, so that each member knows what's happening with each client; and a treasury envelope, in which we keep dues money. (The money goes for things such as a share of Claudia's phone bill and contributions to Charlie's gas fund.) We also have some fun extras, such as Kid-Kits, which are boxes we keep filled with hand-me-down toys and games, plus markers and stickers and things. Kid-Kits are lifesavers on rainy days!

Now, I don't want to sound conceited, so I won't tell you who came up with the idea for Kid-Kits and for all the other things that make the club run so smoothly. I'll just tell you that her initials are K.A.T.

Okay, back to what Claudia was wearing. I'll describe it as best I can, even though I probably don't know all the right names for the things she had on. First of all, she was wearing this blue-and-green stripey shirt that was kind of tight and stretchy-looking. Over it she was wearing a really, really baggy pair of overalls. On her head was a floppy green hat, and on her feet were those big black clunky boots made by Doctor somebody.

She looked great. Claudia has so much style that even *I* can tell she has it. I guess it's part of her extremely artistic nature. Claudia is the most creative person I know. She's not great in school, like her older sister Janine (who happens to be a genius), but it's not because she isn't bright. It's just that she cares more about making the world a more beautiful place than she does about telling the difference between fractions and adverbs.

Claudia's Japanese-American, and very pretty. She has long black hair, almond-shaped eyes, and a perfect complexion. The fact that she is always zit-free is kind of surprising, considering that she practically *lives* on chocolate, potato chips, and various other kinds of junk food (which she has to hide from her disapproving parents, along with the Nancy Drew books they wish she'd outgrow).

Claudia is the BSC's vice-president, mainly because we use her room for meetings. Unlike the rest of us, she has her own phone, with a private line. That really comes in handy during club meetings, when the phone is constantly tied up with calls from clients. Claudia answers the phone during nonmeeting times, but other than that she has no official duties.

"Cool scarf!" I looked up to see Stacey

McGill, Claud's best friend and the BSC's treasurer, entering the room. Naturally, *she* would know the scarf was cool. She has an eye for that kind of thing. I think it's one reason she and Claudia are so close.

I'm in awe of Stacey sometimes. Why? Well, partly because she grew up in New York City, and she seems so much more — I don't know — grown-*up* than the rest of us. She has a cool boyfriend named Robert, who used to be on the SMS basketball team. Stacey dresses like a model, and she looks like one, too, with her long, curly blonde hair and bright blue eyes. Here's what she was wearing that day: platform shoes with really high cork soles (I'm sorry, but I just don't understand why somebody would want to totter around like that), black, lacy legging-things, and a blue dress that looked kind of like these pajamas I used to have when I was seven. Baby dolls, I think they were called.

Stacey's the only child of divorced parents. Her dad lives in an apartment in New York, and while Stacey visits him whenever she can, she lives full-time with her mom in Stoneybrook. (If I were Stacey, I'd use those visits to New York to go to Shea Stadium and see the Mets. Stacey goes to Bloomingdale's instead.) I think the divorce made Stacey grow up in a hurry. That, plus the fact that Stacey has diabetes. She has to take really good care of herself and be very careful about what she eats, because her body doesn't process sugars well. She also has to give herself injections of insulin, which her body *should* make, but doesn't. Stacey deals with her diabetes in an extremely mature way, and I admire her for that.

I also admire the way Stacey keeps the BSC's treasury. Not only does she keep track of how much money she's collected in club dues, she also has a record of every baby-sitting dollar every BSC member has ever earned. It's impressive! But it's second nature for Stacey. She loves math, and always gets A's.

Since it was a Monday, which is dues day, Stacey sat right down on the bed next to Claud and started to busy herself with the manila envelope she uses for the treasury. She was counting a stack of quarters when Mary Anne Spier (my best friend, remember?) walked in.

Mary Anne is the secretary of the BSC, a job which fits her perfectly. She's very neat and precise, and she takes pride in the well-organized record book she keeps. And, like everyone else's, Mary Anne's appearance reflects her personality. She always *looks* very neat and precise. That day, for example, she was wearing a skirt that looked as if she'd ironed it five minutes ago, even though she'd had it on all day, a fresh white shirt, and a red sweater.

The red sweater looked familiar. I recognized it as one she's had for a long, long time. She used to wear it with little-girl jumpers, back when her hair was in pigtails. That wasn't so long ago, either. See, Mary Anne's mom died when Mary Anne (an only child, like Stacey) was just a baby. Mr. Spier brought Mary Anne up on his own, and while I happen to think he did a terrific job (Mary Anne is the sweetest, nicest person I know), maybe he *did* go a little overboard in the strictness department. He had Mary Anne dressing like a ten-year-old well into seventh grade, until she finally stood up to him and put a stop to it. Now Mary Anne has her own sense of style. She even has a cool new haircut these days.

Not only that, Mary Anne has a new sister. That's Dawn Schafer, another member of the BSC and Mary Anne's *other* best friend. (I used to be jealous about that, but I'm over it.) See, after all those years of being a widower, Mr. Spier remarried — and his wife happens to be Dawn's mom, Sharon.

Dawn's mom grew up in Stoneybrook, and she and Mr. Spier dated in high school. Then she went off to California, married somebody else, and had two kids: Dawn and her younger brother Jeff. (Stay with me, now. This is about to get a little confusing!) Eventually, that marriage ended in divorce, and Dawn's mom moved back to Stoneybrook, along with her kids. Jeff never adjusted to life on the east coast, though, and before long he went back to California to live with his dad.

Meanwhile, Mary Anne and Dawn had become friends and discovered that their parents used to date. They reunited them, and the rest is history. Now Dawn, Mary Anne, Richard (that's Mr. Spier), Sharon, and Tigger (Mary Anne's cat) all live in the Schafers' farmhouse.

At least, they all live there most of the time. Not long ago, Dawn was gone for a few months. She'd realized she needed some time with her dad and Jeff, so she went to California for an extended visit. (While she was out there, she gained another family member. Her dad married a woman named Carol, whom Dawn has come to like.)

Now that you know Dawn's entire family history, let me clue you in to what she was wearing that day when she showed up, not long after Mary Anne. She had on a soft, fuzzy brown sweater that looked terrific with her long blonde hair, and cozy-looking white thermal leggings. Like me, Dawn values comfort over anything else when it comes to dressing. *Un*like me, she manages to be comfortable and also display a sense of style.

19

I like Dawn because, again like me, she never hesitates to speak her mind. She doesn't worry too much about what anybody else thinks; she just does her own thing. For example, she's the only club member besides Stacey who never joins in our junk-food binges. While Stacey can't eat the stuff for health reasons, Dawn turns it down because she'd honestly rather eat whole-wheat crackers or an apple.

Dawn is the club's alternate officer, which means she can cover for any other officer who can't make a meeting. While she was in California, that position was held by Shannon Kilbourne, who is normally one of our two associate members. Logan Bruno, Mary Anne's boyfriend, is the other. He and Shannon don't usually come to meetings, but they're on call for the times we're swamped with work.

The last two members to show up for our meeting that day were Jessi Ramsey and Mallory Pike, who are best friends. Here's what they were wearing: Jessi had on a black ballet-leotard top and jeans, with bulky red knitted leg warmers slouched around her ankles. Mal was wearing jeans, a purple sweater, and a big yellow button that said "I Read Banned Books."

What do their outfits tell about them? Well,

Jessi's leotard and leg warmers are clues to the fact that she's a serious ballet dancer, and Mal's button shows that she's a dedicated reader. But there's more to know about both of them. For example, Mal and Jessi are junior officers of the BSC. That's because they're eleven and in the sixth grade (everyone else is thirteen and in the eighth), and they're only allowed to sit at night if it's for their own families.

Speaking of families, Mal has a huge one. She has seven younger brothers and sisters. Jessi, who is African-American, has a smaller, but very close family: her parents, a baby brother, a little sister, and an aunt who lives with them.

Jessi and Mal arrived that afternoon just as I was about to call the meeting to order. I always watch Claudia's digital clock closely, and the second it clicks to five-thirty, I start the meeting, whether everybody's there or not. That day, just as Jessi and Mal were settling into their usual spot on the floor, the clock clicked. "Order!" I said. The word was barely out of my mouth when the phone started to ring. We answered three calls in a row. Mary Anne checked the record book each time and told us who was available for which job. Everything went smoothly, as usual. Until Mrs. Dodson called, that is. She wasn't looking for a baby-sitter. She wanted a *plant*-sitter, to look after her plants while she and her family were in Florida.

"Oh, *no!*" groaned Stacey, who recently took a house-and-pet-sitting job that turned out to be a little more difficult than she'd expected.

"Don't worry, Stace," said Mary Anne, who was checking the record book. "The job won't go to you. In fact, the only person who could take it would be you, Jessi. Since the Dodsons live right down the street from you, you could easily duck in once in a while."

"Okay," said Jessi unenthusiastically. None of us loves sitting jobs that don't involve kids, but we take them anyway. It's good for business. I called Mrs. Dodson back to let her know that Jessi would watch her plants.

"At least the plants won't be climbing the walls the way the kids are doing these days," said Mal. "I think everybody has cabin fever from being cooped up all winter. I know my brothers and sisters do. They're driving me nuts!"

"I know what you mean," said Mary Anne. "I noticed that when I sat for the Rodowskys the other day. They were wilder than ever."

"Well, let's think of some new ways to entertain kids inside," I said, whipping out a notebook. "I'll make a list." After a second, everybody started calling out ideas. That's what I love about the BSC. My friends and I really care about kids and we love the challenge of keeping them happy. As you've seen, we're seven different people, but loving kids and baby-sitting is one thing we have in common!

# CHAPTER 3

I love the term "cabin fever." Oh, I'll admit that the first time I heard it, I was confused. I pictured a hot, sweaty little log cabin with a thermometer in its mouth. Funny image, but as I soon found out, it's not at all what people mean when they talk about having cabin fever.

What they mean is that they feel bored, restless, bored, jumpy, bored, irritable, and cranky. And bored. Bored, most of all. Why? Because it's winter (nobody has cabin fever in the summer) and they haven't been out of the house in weeks. It's been too cold, too icy, too dreary. Sledding's no fun anymore, and everybody's sick of making snow angels. And spring is still weeks and weeks away.

Why am I going into all of this? Simple. The term "cabin fever" is the only one that describes perfectly what was going on in my house on that cold, gray, sleety February afternoon. It was Thursday, a few days after the

BSC meeting I just described. After a long dull day at school, I had come home ready for a fun afternoon of sitting for my siblings (and stepsiblings). Now I normally have a terrific time when I'm watching the four of them. David Michael is sweet and funny, Emily Michelle is cute, Karen is always up to something new, and Andrew is very affectionate.

But that day, there was something in the air. David Michael was in an extremely whiny mood (he's a champion whiner when he really gets going), Andrew was feeling cranky, Karen was being bossy, and Emily Michelle just wanted to be left alone to suck her thumb, which is not something she normally does.

Cabin fever? You bet.

And the worst part was this: the one thing I haven't mentioned about cabin fever is that it's catching. So even though I had been looking forward to the afternoon, it wasn't long before the fever took *me* over, too. Within minutes, I felt just as cranky, whiny, and bossy as everybody else. (I *did* draw the line at sucking my thumb.) I tried to hide my feelings, though. After all, as a baby-sitter, I was supposed to represent the adult world. It's okay to act like a kid for fun when you're sitting. In fact, you'll have a much better time if you just join in any games that are going on. But it's not okay to act childish in negative ways.

So, instead of stamping my foot or sticking out my lower lip or starting a "did too," "did not" fight, I decided to rise above my cabin fever. I looked around at my four grouchy charges and tried to figure out how to distract them.

Here's what they were doing: David Michael was sitting on the couch. He had folded his arms across his chest and stuck out his lower lip so far somebody could have tripped on it. "I *hate* winter," he was saying. "Why can't it be spring? Why can't we live someplace where it's always warm? I'm sick of winter . . ." He went on and on and on. Meanwhile, Karen was trying to force the younger kids into playing house with her. "You have to be the baby," she told Emily Michelle in a bossy voice. "And you be the father," she ordered Andrew. "I'm the mommy. Ready?"

Andrew just shook his head. "No thanks," he said. Karen frowned at him, and then turned to Emily Michelle and tried to pick her up as if she were an infant.

"No. No! NO!" cried Emily. "Puddown! Puddown!"

"Karen," I said, trying to keep the edge out of my voice. "She wants you to put her down."

"No, she *likes* being the baby," Karen insisted, still trying to lift Emily. But she had to shout to make herself heard, because Emily was wailing so loudly.

"I don't think so," I said. "You really need to put her down. Now."

Karen let Emily drop — hard. Emily's wails turned to shrieks. "Karen Brewer!" I said as I ran over to make sure Emily was okay. "You go sit in that chair. You're in Time Out."

Karen flounced over to Watson's big easy chair and flung herself into it. She folded her arms and stuck out her lip until she looked just like David Michael. Meanwhile, I was checking out Emily. "You're okay," I told her. "That was just a little bump, and it scared you. But you're okay." I knelt on the floor and hugged her until her cries died down.

Then Andrew started whimpering. "What's the matter?" I asked him. He didn't answer. "I guess you need a hug, too," I said, gathering him into my arms. His whimpering stopped as soon as I was holding him, so I knew I'd guessed right. I think he sometimes misses being the baby of the family.

I sat down on the couch, Andrew still in my arms. I looked around at everyone and took a breath. "Okay, you guys," I said. "Listen up. I know you're tired of being cooped up inside. How about if we think of something fun to do, instead of just sitting around being crabby?"

"Fine," said David Michael. His arms were still folded across his chest. "Like what?"

"Yeah," added Karen. "Like what? Can we play Let's All Come In?"

"No *way*!" said David Michael. He turned to me. "Right, Kristy? No way, right?"

"Well," I said, trying to be diplomatic. Let's All Come In is a game of make-believe that Karen made up, and she *loves* to play it. But David Michael can't stand it. "Maybe we should try to think of something we'd *all* enjoy."

"Fine," said Karen, echoing David Michael.

"Fine," said Andrew.

"Fide!" said Emily Michelle, copying Karen's and David Michael's arms-folded-across-the-chest posture.

*"Like what?"* they all asked together.

I thought of the list we'd made at Monday's BSC meeting. "Well, how about a singalong?" I asked brightly. David Michael rolled his eyes. "Or we could play school, or store!" I was trying to sound enthusiastic. I saw Karen's eyes brighten at the thought of a game of let's pretend, but none of the other kids seemed interested. I plowed ahead. "Want to make origami figures?" I asked. "Have a marching band? Make collages? How about if we start planning this summer's garden? What about writing and making our own books?" No, no, no, no, and no. Not one of those ideas seemed to excite the kids.

I tried not to feel hurt. After all, some of those ideas had been mine, and all of them had been good ones.

I tried a couple more. "How about playing Old Maid, or Go Fish? What if we make Play-Doh?" But cabin fever had hit hard at the Thomas-Brewer house that day. The kids could not — or *would* not — agree on an activity.

"I know!" said Karen suddenly. "Let's go play in Daddy's library. He has lots of cool old stuff, and he always tells me it's okay to explore in there."

Now, don't ask me why, but for some reason everybody loved that idea. It didn't seem all that much better than all the ideas *I'd* offered, but you know what? I wasn't really hurt. All I cared about was that the kids had agreed on something to do. "Great," I said, when I saw everybody nodding enthusiastically. "Let's go!"

Watson's library is a dark, peaceful, comfortable place, with cushy leather chairs, thick rugs, china lamps, a big wooden desk, and, of course, shelves and shelves full of books. The room has a nice smell to it; that special library smell made up of musty books, lemon furniture polish, and something else. Ink, maybe? Or glue? Anyway, that smell always makes me want to grab a book and a blanket and curl up to read for hours and hours.

Emily Michelle clambered up into one of the leather chairs and then slid back off it. "Whee!" she said. Andrew joined her at the game. Meanwhile, Karen and David Michael poked around, looking at the books. David Michael had climbed up on the wood-and-brass stepladder and was gazing at the titles on a higher shelf, while Karen scooted along on the floor, looking at the books on the bottom shelf.

"Boy, some of these books are really old!" said Karen.

"I know," I said. I've looked through Watson's library before.

"What's the oldest book in here?" David Michael asked me. "I bet you can't find it."

"Bet I can," I said. I started to scan the shelves, looking for faded old covers. It didn't take me long to find one that looked pretty ancient. I pulled it off the shelf and blew some dust off it. "I don't know if this is the *oldest* one," I said. "But it's old, all right. And it's about Stoneybrook!" The title of the book was *The Stoneybrooke Town Record*, and it was dated 1864.

"Cool!" said David Michael. "Let's see!"

I sat down on the love seat with Karen and

David Michael. (Andrew and Emily had decided to lie down on the big couch, put an afghan over themselves, and "play nap." But within moments they weren't just playing. They were fast asleep.) I opened the book and started to flip through the pages. "It's in sections," I said. "This first part is like an almanac, with all the historical stuff arranged by date."

"Ha!" said David Michael, pointing to an entry. " 'April 8, 1832: Amos Murphy's best cow has been stolen.' Guess they thought that was big news back then."

"Look at this one," I said. " 'July 2, 1826: The widow Jones reports that a neighbor's hog has destroyed her dahlias.' " I laughed. "Sounds like a crime wave."

"What's the other section?" asked Karen.

"It's a directory of people who lived in Stoneybrook back then," I said. "Arranged by name."

"Look up Thomas," urged David Michael. "Maybe we have some famous ancestors."

I turned some pages, looking for the T's. When I found them, I ran my finger down the list. Then suddenly, my finger stopped. "Whoa!" I said, looking at one of the entries.

"That's spooky," said David Michael, who had seen it, too.

"Her name's almost like yours," said Karen,

who was leaning over to read along with us.

All three of us were staring at this entry: "Christina Thomas. Born September 7, 1845. Date of death unknown. Daughter of Rachel and John Thomas (both d. 1861) of Squirelot. Disappeared January 1863, under mysterious circumstances."

"Oooh," said Karen, drawing in a breath. "She *disappeared*?"

"I wonder if she's our ancestor," said David Michael.

Christina Thomas. Her name really was a lot like mine. A chill ran down my spine, and suddenly I had this wonderful feeling. Cabin fever? Forget about it. I had a mystery to solve.

# CHAPTER 4

"Any other new business?" I asked, hoping very much that there wasn't. I gazed around Claudia's room at my friends. It was Friday, at five-forty-five, and we were in the middle of a BSC meeting. I couldn't *wait* to tell my friends about the mystery I'd come across the day before, but I had to. Wait, that is. Why? Well, because I sort of have this rule for BSC meetings: Club business always comes first. If members have other things they want to talk about after we've taken care of club business, that's fine. But they have to wait.

It's a good rule. It really is. But this one time I *hated* the fact that, as president, I absolutely had to follow it. I was dying to spill my news. I hadn't even told Mary Anne yet. I was waiting until I could tell everybody at once. Waiting, and waiting, and waiting. I was starting to wish I'd never made up that stupid rule about BSC business.

Usually there isn't much business to take care of, but wouldn't you know it? At *this* meeting, there was a ton. It seemed as though everybody had a client they needed advice about, or a problem with scheduling, or a report to make. Like Jessi's.

"I wanted to report on my plant-sitting job," she said. (This was *after* we'd gone through all the other club business, answered three phone calls, and assigned the jobs. I was dying.)

"I think I must have whatever the *opposite* of a green thumb is," Jessi was saying. "I've only been taking care of Mrs. Dodson's plants for a few days, and already some of them are beginning to droop. A couple of them look wilted, too. And I keep having to pick yellow leaves off one of them."

"Maybe they always look like that," Stacey suggested.

Jessi shook her head. "I wish," she said. "Unfortunately, they don't. Mrs. Dodson is really, *really* good with plants. When she first showed me around, I couldn't believe how healthy they all looked. The plants in our house only look that good on the first day we bring them home!"

"Same here," Mal put in, laughing. She gave Jessi a sympathetic look.

"Did Mrs. Dodson leave you instructions?" Mary Anne asked Jessi.

"Three pages worth." She has all these routines for each plant. She puts a lot of energy into caring for those things. It's like they were pets or children, or something."

"Well, is there anything in the instructions that might help?" Claudia asked.

Shaking her head, Jessi said, "I've read them over and over again until I've practically memorized them. And I'm following them to the letter. But nothing seems to help."

I was still eager to talk about my mystery, but I have to admit I was a little distracted by Jessi's problem. "If Mrs. Dodson comes home and finds her plants dead, that's not going to look too good for the BSC," I said. I was imagining Mrs. Dodson telling everybody she knows that the BSC members are plant-killers. I hate the thought of anybody spreading negative information about us. We could start losing clients.

"We should find somebody who knows about plants, so we can ask him," Dawn said. "But who?"

We were quiet for a minute. Then Mal sat up straight. "I know!" she said. "What about the arboretum? There must be somebody there who could help."

"Arboretum?" I asked. "Isn't that one of those places where they keep plant specimens? I didn't know there even *was* one around here."

"I didn't know either," said Mal, "but my sister's class just went there on a field trip. It's right on the outskirts of town. It's a small place, but Vanessa said the woman who runs it is really friendly. I bet she'll help."

"Great!" said Jessi. She looked relieved. "I'll try to go there this weekend."

"Okay," I said. "That's all taken care of. Any other new business?" By that time our meeting was almost over, and I still hadn't had a chance to tell everybody about Christina Thomas.

My friends shook their heads. "Good," I said. "There's something I want — "

"Ooh, ooh, I forgot," said Claudia, waving her hand. "I *do* have some new business." She dug around under her pillow (one of her favorite junk food hiding places) and pulled out a cellophane bag. "These are new," she said, holding the bag up. "Cocoa Blinkens. Has anybody tried them yet? They're terrific."

"Um, Claud, I don't exactly think a new kind of candy is club business," I pointed out.

She looked deflated. "Does that mean you don't want to try one?" she asked, holding out the bag hopefully.

"Well . . ." I said. "Just this once." I grinned as I stuck my hand into the bag and pulled out a couple of candies. Claud passed the bag to the others, and everyone except Dawn and Stacey took a few.

"You're right, Claud. These are great," I said. "And now, I have something *I* want to discuss."

"But Kristy," Mary Anne began.

"But nothing," I snapped. "I've waited patiently all this time, and now it's my turn."

I was ready to go on, but Mary Anne looked so hurt I gave in.

"Okay, Mary Anne, what is it?" I asked.

She didn't say anything. Instead, she just pointed to the clock on Claud's nightstand. It was six o'clock. Our meeting was over.

"I can't believe it!" I said. "Now I'll *never* have the chance to tell you guys about the mystery I stumbled across."

"Mystery?" Mal asked, looking interested.

"Really? A mystery?" asked Dawn. "We don't mind staying a few minutes later. Do we, guys?"

"Mind? Are you kidding? Tell us everything," said Claudia, leaning forward to listen.

Everybody in the BSC *loves* mysteries.

"Well, okay. But first, there's one thing I have to do," I said, teasing them a little. It's always fun to have an audience in the palm of your hand.

"What?" Stacey asked impatiently.

"Adjourn the meeting!" I said, giggling.

Claudia threw a pillow at me. "So adjourn it, already."

"Okay, this meeting is hereby adjourned," I said in a rush. "Now, on to the important stuff —"

The next day, I began my research. Telling my friends about Christina had only made me more excited about exploring the mystery of who she was, why she had disappeared, and whether she was related to me. Together, we'd decided that the next step would be to do some fact-finding at the Stoneybrook Public Library.

As it turned out, I was the only BSC member who didn't have a sitting job that Saturday morning. (Actually, Stacey didn't have a job, either. She had plans to spend the day with Robert.) I was at the library all by myself. I missed my friends, especially Claud, who is great at using microfilm.

Mrs. Kishi (Claudia's mom, who is head librarian) wasn't at work that morning, but there was a really helpful assistant librarian on duty, and he set me up with the microfilm for old issues of the *Stoneybrook News*, which was where my friends and I had decided I should start my research. The library has the newspaper on microfilm going back all the way to 1820, so I knew that if I looked carefully, I should be able to find *some* information about the Thomas family.

My friends thought my find in the *Stoneybrooke Town Record* was a great one. They were as curious as I was about Christina, and they promised to help me look into the mystery as soon as they had some time. But not that morning.

It took me a while to figure out how to use the index of the newspaper. Then, when I started looking through the actual articles, I kept getting distracted by interesting stuff about historical Stoneybrook. For example, I never knew there used to be a movie theatre where the supermarket is now. Or that there was once a bakery next door to Bellair's department store.

Finally, I realized that if I kept browsing aimlessly I wasn't going to find *any* information about the Thomases. I started to concentrate on scanning for articles about that family.

It wasn't long before I hit pay dirt. The first article I found was about Christina's parents, John and Rachel Thomas. And what the article said was so, so sad. In 1861, they died together in a freak carriage accident.

I checked the scrap of paper on which I'd

written down the information I already knew about Christina. According to her birthdate, she would have been only sixteen when that happened. Poor Christina.

The accident made her rich, though. Her parents' estate, according to the next article I found, was divided among Christina (the oldest child), and her brothers Devon and Edward.

But the last article I found about Christina was the most interesting. It was about her disappearance in January 1863. There wasn't any real information about where she might have gone, or why, but one sentence in the story caught my eye:

"Authorities report that, according to her brother Edward (the last Stoneybrook resident to see her), a small fortune in gold, as well as documents representing a share of the Thomas family holdings, disappeared with Miss Thomas."

I turned my face away from the microfilm reader and gazed up at the ceiling, to give my eyes — and my brain — a rest. Then I looked back and read it again. I could hardly believe what I was seeing.

If Christina *was* a relative of mine, that missing fortune might make more than just a good story and a fun mystery. It might make me rich.

# CHAPTER 5

Saturday

No more February doldrums! I've found a great new project for the BSC. It's something we can do with the kids, something that will distract them — and us — from these last few yucky weeks of winter. We'll be helping someone out, and we might learn a few things along the way. My thumb may even end up turning green, after all!

Jessi's entry in the BSC notebook was a little mysterious, but it didn't take long for the rest of us to find out what she was talking about. And when we did, we were just as enthusiastic as she was about the new project.

It started on Saturday morning, the same Saturday morning I was spending at the library. Jessi had a sitting job with Charlotte Johanssen, who's one of the BSC's favorite charges. (She's a *special* favorite of Stacey's — they consider each other "almost sisters.") Charlotte is eight years old and pretty, with chestnut brown hair, big, dark eyes, and this dimple that only shows up when she smiles. She's very smart — she skipped into third grade not long ago — and very sweet, and just a little bit shy.

Jessi's always had a special liking for Charlotte, because she was the first kid in Stoneybrook to make friends with Jessi's sister, Becca. See, when the Ramseys first moved here from New Jersey, they went through a tough time. There aren't all that many African-American families in Stoneybrook, and at first people didn't seem to know how to act around the Ramseys. (Well, some people thought they knew how to act: mean and horrible. But most people just held back and weren't overly friendly.)

But Charlotte didn't see any reason not to make friends with Becca. After all, they were the same age. They both loved to read. And Becca is just the littlest bit shy herself. So Charlotte stepped forward and made friends with Becca, and ever since then they've been very close.

Which was one of the reasons Jessi had invited Charlotte over to *her* house that Saturday morning, instead of sitting for her at the Johanssens'. Becca had been moping around the Ramsey house, and Jessi recognized cabin fever when she saw it. She knew it was a good bet that Charlotte had a touch of the fever, too.

Sure enough, as soon as Charlotte arrived, the girls began moping together. "There's nothing to *do*," said Becca.

"I'm *bored*," said Charlotte.

"Maybe Squirt will let us dress him up like a clown again," said Becca halfheartedly. The girls had resorted to playing dress-up with Squirt the last time they were together.

"I don't think so," Jessi said quickly. As she remembered it, Squirt hadn't had quite as much fun as the girls had, during that particular game.

"Well, what *can* we do, then?" asked Becca.

Jessi looked out the window. The sky wasn't exactly blue, but it wasn't totally gray, either.

And it wasn't sleeting, for a change. "You know, it's not that cold out today," she said. "We could play outside."

"But there's hardly any snow left," said Becca. "We can't go sledding."

Jessi was beginning to feel exasperated. But just then, Charlotte said something that gave her an idea.

"I wish spring would come," said Charlotte. "I can't wait to see everything turn green."

"Green!" said Jessi, snapping her fingers. "That's it!"

"What?" chorused the girls.

"I just figured out what we can do. Hold on for a second while I ask Dad if he'll drive us somewhere." Jessi ran to find her father, and a few minutes later she was calling to Becca and Charlotte, "Put your jackets on. We're going to the arboretum."

"Arbor-what?" asked Charlotte.

"What's that?" asked Becca.

"Arboretum. It's a place where they have all kinds of plants," said Jessi. "I was planning to go there sometime this weekend, and this seems like the perfect time. I think you two will like it there." She crossed her fingers as she said this. As she told me later, she had no idea what to expect at the arboretum, and she didn't know if the girls would like it or not. But she couldn't think of anything else to do, and she figured a field trip just might cure their winter blues.

Half an hour later, Jessi and the girls stood on a tree-lined, semicircular gravel driveway, looking up at a gigantic old red brick house. It was three stories high, with lots of huge windows trimmed in white. There was a very formal-looking front entrance, with broad steps leading to a small porch with an arched roof and wide white columns on either side.

Mr. Ramsey hadn't wanted to drop them off without waiting to see them go in, but Jessi told him they'd be fine. "The sign on the front gate said they're open," she'd pointed out. "And there's a gas station right down the street. We can call you from there when we need a ride home."

As Jessi and the girls walked closer to the house, they could see that there was an old-fashioned greenhouse built onto the left wing. Through the steamed-up glass they saw glimpses of bright red and pink.

"Ooh, pretty," said Charlotte. "Do we get to go in there?"

"Probably," said Jessi. "Let's go inside and find out about this place, okay?" Suddenly, she felt a little shy. She'd never walked into a house as fancy as this one. (Watson's mansion is big, but nowhere *near* as grand.) But she screwed up her courage and, with the girls following behind her, climbed the steps to the entrance. There was no doorbell, and no knocker. Jessi reached out tentatively to try the doorknob, and the door swung open, surprising her. She stepped back, but Becca and Charlotte walked right in.

"Why, hello, girls!" A gray-haired woman wearing a bright pink smock over jeans and a white shirt smiled up at them. She was crouched on the black-and-white-tiled floor of the entryway, clipping dead leaves from a huge plant that was really more like a small tree. "Welcome to the arboretum."

"Um, thanks," said Jessi. She wasn't quite sure what to make of this woman. Was she the owner? Or a custodian, or what?

The woman straightened up. "I'm Mrs. Goldsmith, the curator," she explained, as if she'd read Jessi's mind. "I look after the place, or at least, I try to! It's a big job." She laughed and wiped her forehead with a gloved hand, leaving a dirty smudge across her face. "Did you want a tour? Or would you just like to look around on your own?"

"We'd love a tour," said Jessi. "Right, girls?" The girls nodded, looking a little shy. Jessi still felt a bit overwhelmed herself. In fact, she'd almost forgotten the purpose of her visit.

46

Suddenly, she remembered that she had come to ask about Mrs. Dodson's plants. But, she admitted to me later, she didn't feel comfortable asking for help right away. Instead, she decided to ask *after* the tour.

So Jessi and the girls followed Mrs. Goldsmith as she led them through a huge but basically empty living room and toward the greenhouse.

"Who lives here?" asked Becca. "Do you?"

"My goodness, no!" said Mrs. Goldsmith. "Little old me in this gigantic place?" She laughed. "No, nobody lives here. In fact, we have the upstairs pretty much closed off these days. There's no point in paying to heat this whole house." Just then, she reached the greenhouse door. She pulled it open, and, as Jessi told me later, a cloud of sweet-smelling, warm air seemed to draw all four of them into the steamy, bright room.

"Wow!" said Charlotte, looking around in awe. "This is so, so cool."

Mrs. Goldsmith smiled. "I'm glad you like it," she said. "I spend most of my days in here. It *is* wonderful, isn't it?"

They stood there, gazing happily at the sight of all those green, growing things and drinking in the feeling of warmth. The room was full of plants: plants on shelves, plants on the floor, plants climbing up trellises along the glass walls. Their leaves were all shades of green, and many of them were blooming. Jessi spotted the red and pink flowers they'd seen from outside and asked what they were.

"Geraniums," said Mrs. Goldsmith, leading them to the flowers for a closer look. She leaned over and sniffed a red one. "Don't you love the way they smell? Kind of musty and spicy. I adore it."

After everyone had sniffed the geraniums, Mrs. Goldsmith led them around and showed them the other plants. Then they headed back inside. As they walked through the living room, Jessi glanced out of a large window and saw the property in back of the house. She saw a tangle of shrubs and vines, and what once must have been formal gardens — with statues, a gazebo, and a fountain — that looked as if they hadn't been tended in quite some time. She asked Mrs. Goldsmith about it.

"It's such a shame," said the curator, shaking her head. "Underneath the mess, those gardens are a real historical treasure. There are plants in there that you can't find anywhere else these days, even though they originated in this area. The gardens were started over a hundred years ago." She sighed. "And now the arboretum is on the brink of closing."

"What?" asked Jessi. "Why?"

"Well," said Mrs. Goldsmith, "the house and the greenhouse belong to Stoneybrook, but that land out there probably doesn't. We aren't sure *who* it belongs to, since the original lease for it is missing and the town records were destroyed in a fire years and years ago. Now the land has caught the eye of a developer who wants to build subdivisions here. He brought the question of the lease to the state's attention, and now the state is planning to auction the land off." She paused. "If the land is sold, the arboretum will have to close. We can barely afford to keep it open as it is, and without the fees we charge for summer garden tours we'd be lost. Anyway, if he buys the land, the developer will have the right to kick us out and knock down the house."

"That's awful!" said Jessi. She was horrified.

"Isn't there anything you can *do* about it?" asked Charlotte.

"Well, we do have one hope," said Mrs. Goldsmith, though she didn't sound too hopeful. "There's a wealthy donor, Mrs. VanderBellen, who's expressed some interest in buying the land and maintaining the arboretum. She's supposed to be coming by one day soon to look the place over." The curator glanced out the window, and Jessi followed her gaze. Then Mrs. Goldsmith shook her head. "But I'm afraid I'll never be able to whip this place into decent shape in time," she said. "Not without my summer help. They're all college students, so I won't have them until June."

That was when Jessi had her great idea. She started talking without having thought it out, but Mrs. Goldsmith just listened and nodded. And before long, they'd worked out all the details:

Jessi, and whatever kids and BSC members she could round up, would volunteer after-school time to help clean up the arboretum grounds. In return, Mrs. Goldsmith would help Jessi figure out what to do with Mrs. Dodson's ailing plants. (Actually, Mrs. Goldsmith told Jessi she would have been glad to do that in any case. But Jessi insisted that this arrangement was a fair exchange.)

Soon after, Jessi called her dad and asked him to pick her and the girls up. And all the way home, the three of them chattered happily about how much fun it would be to fix up the arboretum, and maybe — just maybe — save it from the developers. Jessi was sure she'd finally come up with the perfect cure for cabin fever.

# CHAPTER 6

"It sounds like fun. But what if we pull up some hundred-year-old specimen by mistake? All those plant things look the same to me." Stacey looked perplexed.

"*Plant* things?" asked Claud, cracking up. "Oh, Stacey, you're such a city girl." Then she lost her grin. "Come to think of it, I don't know that much about plants myself," she added. She dug into the bowl of popcorn she held on her lap and pulled out a handful. Then she passed the bowl to Stacey.

It was Monday, and we were in the midst of our BSC meeting. We had already taken care of all the club business, and now we were discussing Jessi's idea for helping to save the arboretum. I was interested in the project, but once again I was waiting to bring up my own subject: the mystery of Christina. So, I listened to the conversation going on around me, but at the same time I was thinking about my mystery, and about the best way to present the facts to my friends. I chewed nervously on my pencil while I waited.

"Mrs. Goldsmith said it wouldn't matter whether we knew anything about gardening or not," said Jessi, in answer to Stacey and Claud. "She'll tell us exactly what to do. Anyway, it's really too cold for weeding and taking care of plants. We're just trying to make the place look decent. There's a lot of litter to be picked up and hauled away, and stone walls to be repaired, and raking to do — stuff like that. Mrs. Goldsmith also needs help cataloging the indoor plants and tidying up the greenhouse."

"I usually hate gardening," said Mal. "But I'm so sick of winter it actually sounds like fun."

"I know," I said, putting down my gnawed-up pencil and forgetting about Christina for a minute. "Maybe I'll take Karen and David Michael there on Thursday. They'd have a great time."

"I won't be able to get there for a few days," said Mary Anne. "But I'm sitting for the Arnold twins on Friday so I'll definitely bring them over. They love projects like this." Then Mary Anne turned to me with an odd look on her face. "Kristy, why are you jiggling your leg like that? Are you nervous about something?"

"Me, jiggling?" I asked, surprised. Trust Mary Anne to notice.

"Yes," she said. "And just look at your pencil."

Mary Anne sounded so much like my third-grade teacher that I had to giggle. I held up the pencil and looked at it. "Delicious," I said.

"So, what's up?" asked Mary Anne.

"Oh, nothing much," I said, trying to act casual. "Just that I might be a millionaire if I can solve this mystery." I raised my eyebrows and pretended to yawn.

"A *millionaire*?" asked Mary Anne. Her mouth had fallen open.

"What are you talking about?" asked Dawn.

"Spill the beans!" said Jessi.

"Well, you remember Christina Thomas, right?" I asked. "The girl who disappeared? The one we thought might possibly be related to me?"

Everybody nodded. "Go on," said Stacey.

"Well, I found out yesterday that at the time she disappeared, Christina was very rich," I said, drawing it out. Why not add a little suspense?

"And?" asked Claudia, giving me a threatening look.

"And her fortune disappeared with her," I said. "As far as I could tell, it's never been found."

"Whoa!" breathed Claudia.

"A missing fortune," mused Mal. "What a great story!"

It sounded as if Mal were already plotting a children's book about this mystery. The only problem was that we hadn't solved it yet.

"You could be rich," said Stacey dreamily. "I mean, I know Watson's rich, but this would be your own money. Just think, you could be wearing original Gaultier clothes and jewelry from Tiffany's."

"Uh, right," I said. I had no idea who Goat-ee-ay was, but I had the feeling I wouldn't wear his clothes if I had *three* million dollars to spend. And as for jewels from Tiffany's, I'd rather have a new first-baseman's mitt by Rawlings. "There's only one problem," I added. "Or rather, make that two." I held up two fingers and counted off the reasons. "One: I don't know where Christina disappeared to. And two: I don't know how or where to find her fortune." I held up one more finger. "Not to mention a third problem: I don't have any way of knowing if she really is related to me, anyway."

"Hmmm," said Claudia. She dug into the popcorn bowl again, absently. She was staring off into space, her brow wrinkled.

I could almost *see* Claud's brain working. She has read every single Nancy Drew book in existence (some of them twice), and she remembers every single mystery and how it was solved. (Don't ask me why she can't remember enough to pass a weekly math quiz.)

"Sounds like you need to do a little more digging," Claudia finally said.

"But where?" I asked.

"Back at the library," said Claud, holding up a finger. "I'll help. We'll have to look through some of the old town records they keep there."

"I'll help, too," said Mary Anne. "Let's go tomorrow, after school. We can go through all the old newspapers on file, too."

I groaned.

"It won't be so bad, with three of us working," Claudia reassured me. "Besides, isn't it worth it? You might be earning yourself a fortune!"

"Right," I said. "And I suppose you'll want a share of it, too."

"You know it," she said, laughing. "Shall we say, oh, fifty-fifty?"

"What about me?" asked Mary Anne. "I'm helping, too."

"Oh, right," said Claud. "So we'll each make — let's see, how much is three into a million dollars?" She pretended to punch some numbers into a calculator. We all cracked up.

As soon as school was over the next day, I headed for the library with Mary Anne and Claudia. We were each carrying notebooks and pens, and I had a file I'd made which contained the information I had found so far.

Mrs. Kishi greeted us when we trooped in. "Nice to see you, girls," she said. "I have you set up in the reference room. If you can use any help on your school project, just let me know."

School project? Automatically, I thanked Mrs. Kishi. But as soon as her back was turned, I raised my eyebrows at Claudia.

She shrugged. "I didn't think she'd be crazy about me wasting my time pretending to be Nancy Drew," she explained. "So I fibbed just a little."

"*Claudia!*" said Mary Anne.

"*Claudia!*" I echoed.

"What?" Claudia asked innocently. "Let's start working. What are we waiting for?" She led us to the reference room, where Mrs. Kishi had left out stacks of microfilm and piles of old books. "Yikes," said Claudia, when she saw how much material we had to go through.

"You know, now that I think about it, there's this new book on Matisse my mom told me about. Maybe I'll go look for it."

"And I wanted to find a craft book. I need some ideas for making cat toys," said Mary Anne. They both started to edge away.

"Oh, no, you don't," I said. "I have other stuff I could do here, too. I promised David Michael I'd look up some stats in the *Baseball Encyclopedia*. But we have a job to do. Let's just get it over with!"

After that, we settled down to work, and I have to say we made a pretty terrific team. Claudia flipped through the microfilm index to the *Stoneybrook News*, and called out the numbers for pages that might give us information we needed. I took down the numbers in my notebook and lined up the rolls of microfilm we'd need to look at. Mary Anne, meanwhile, began to pore over the town records, running a finger down each page and taking notes on any Thomas connections that looked as if they might be important.

Most of the work was boring and repetitive and frustrating. Tracing a family history may seem simple, but it isn't. For one thing, people move away, and then sometimes turn up again. Also, daughters get married and change their names. Not every Thomas descendent was a Thomas. Far from it. We ended up having to trace the Johnson and Abbott families, too.

We did find out a few interesting things. For example, we read the details of the carriage accident in which Christina's parents died (it was as gruesome as a modern-day car wreck). Plus, we found out a *little* bit more about Christina's disappearance. Apparently, she had left Squirelot, her parents' estate, on or about January 8th of 1863. A scullery maid insisted that Christina had been headed for Pennsylvania, but no trace of her was ever found in that state or in any town between it and Stoneybrook.

As for tracing the Thomas descendents, we ran into a lot of dead ends. John and Rachel had had three children: Christina, Devon, and Edward. Christina, of course, had disappeared. Devon had a son, Devon II and *he* had a son, Devon III. Devon III had also had a son (guess what his name is!), but from what we could tell he wasn't a Stoneybrook resident.

Edward, meanwhile, had *three* children: Scott, Mary, and Ellen. Mary never had children, and Ellen's children wouldn't have been Thomases, so I figured Scott was the ony one who could be my ancestor. I even had a vague memory of my dad telling me about his great-great-aunt Mary, who'd never married. For a few minutes I was pretty excited about finding a link that would tie me to Christina's fortune. So were Mary Anne and Claudia. The only problem was that we couldn't find a single descendent of Scott's listed in the Stoneybrook records or mentioned in the newspaper. See what I mean about dead ends?

After about three hours in the library, we came up with a family tree that looked something like this:

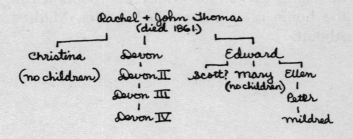

We traced Ellen Thomas's descendents (who seemed to be the only members of the family to stay in Stoneybrook) down to a woman named Mildred Abbott. Mrs. Abbott would be Christina's great-great-niece, if our calculations were right. And according to the phone book, she still lived in Stoneybrook. Other than Mildred, though, the trail was cold.

"So what do we do now?" asked Mary Anne, who was staring down at the Thomas family tree. She looked a little discouraged.

"I know what *I'm* going to do," I told her. "As soon as I get home, I'm going to call this Mrs. Abbott. It looks like she's our only hope. If she doesn't know something about Christina, nobody does. Or at least, nobody we can *find*."

And that's how I, Kristy Thomas, ended up being invited to Friday afternoon tea at the home of — guess who? — Mrs. Mildred Abbott.

# CHAPTER 7

I don't usually waste time being nervous about things; I just do them. That's why I hadn't been tense when I called Mrs. Abbott. I just picked up the phone and called her. When she answered, I told her who I was and why I was interested in talking with her. And she invited me to tea on the spot.

See how easy these things are? There's no reason to be nervous.

But guess what? The second I hung up, I started to feel nervous. Very, very nervous. Why? Well, because Mrs. Abbott sounded like a proper person. The kind of person who might correct your grammar, or tell you to sit up straight and stop slouching. The kind of person who would probably disapprove if I showed up for tea in my usual "uniform" of jeans, running shoes, and a turtleneck.

I wanted to make a good impression on Mrs. Abbott, because from what I could tell by the research we'd done so far, I was going to have to convince her to answer some questions if I wanted to find out more about the Thomas family history. That's why I ended up staring into my closet that night, trying to figure out which of my skirts I could stand to wear. (I only have a couple of them, since I wear them so infrequently.) I chose a dark-green corduroy skirt, which I planned to wear with a white button-down shirt, and a blue sweater, panty hose (ugh!), and brown loafers. I knew I'd catch a lot of teasing when I wore that outfit to school on Friday (since nobody *ever* sees me dressed like that), but I had no choice. I wouldn't have time to go home and change before tea with Mrs. Abbott.

I made sure the clothes I was planning to wear were clean and pressed, and that the loafers were polished. I checked to see that I had a fresh notebook and a working pen, so I'd be ready to take notes on what Mrs. Abbott told me. And I practiced sitting up straight and saying "No, thank you, ma'am," and "yes, please, ma'am."

After that, there was nothing I could do but wait.

Tea wasn't until Friday, so I still had all day Thursday to wait through. School was enough of a distraction, but how would I fill the time after school?

I shouldn't have worried.

After school on Thursday, I stood in front of my closet, doing one more check on my outfit for Friday. Suddenly, there was a knock on my door, and before I could even call out "come in," Karen was bouncing on my bed. "When are we going?" she asked.

"Going?" I said, confused.

"To the plant place!" Karen said. "You promised!"

I had totally forgotten I'd promised to take her and David Michael to the arboretum that day. (That just goes to show you how nervous I was about tea with Mrs. Abbott. Normally, I would *never* forget a promise I'd made to a kid.)

Karen was all psyched up for working at the arboretum. She'd already changed into a pair of overalls and begged Watson to let her borrow his good English trowel. She had David Michael excited about our trip, too.

It's not as if either of them loves gardening that much. Oh, they'll putter around in the garden with Watson, as he trims his roses or mulches his shrubs, but only if there's nothing else to do.

"Nothing else to do" were the key words that day. I knew Karen was only dying to go to the "plant place" because she was so tired of being cooped up in the house.

Well, I felt the same way. I had a little touch of cabin fever myself, not to mention a case of nerves. And a trip to the arboretum seemed the perfect solution.

Watson was happy to drive us there. "I've never even *heard* of this place before," he said when he pulled up to the big brick building. "Isn't this something! I wish I could stay and help, but I have a very important date with a certain young lady." He turned to smile at Emily Michelle, who was strapped into her car seat.

"Barn — ee!" she squealed, waving her hands in the air.

"That's right," said Watson. "We're going to watch Barney together, just as soon as we get home."

I'm still not used to Watson being home so much, but it's obvious that he and Emily Michelle are closer than ever since he's been playing "Mr. Mom." Karen and David Michael and I piled out of the van and waved as Watson and Emily Michelle drove off. Then we set out to find Jessi.

I heard the sound of raking coming from behind the house, so instead of heading inside, we decided to check there first.

"Hey!" I heard Jessi call, as we rounded the corner. "Look who's here." She put down her rake and tapped Matt Braddock, who was raking next to her, on the shoulder. Matt hadn't heard us coming, because he's deaf. He communicates by reading lips and by using American Sign Language. All of the members of the BSC have learned a little ASL — except for Jessi, who's learned a lot. Plus, quite a few of the kids who know Matt have picked up some signs.

David Michael, for example. As soon Matt looked up and saw him David Michael started signing. Matt nodded enthusiastically in response, and pointed toward a nearby shed.

"What did you ask him?" I asked David Michael.

"Just if I could help," he said. "I think he's telling me that there are more rakes in the shed. Should I go get a few?"

"Definitely," I said, and David Michael ran off. It was a chilly day, and raking seemed like the perfect way to warm up, as long as we were going to be working outside. It didn't look like a huge raking job, either. Just a quick cleanup.

"I *hate* raking," said Karen.

"Maybe you'd like to work with Haley, then," suggested Jessi. "She's in the greenhouse with Mrs. Goldsmith, helping to catalog plants."

"All right!" said Karen. "I've been wanting to see that greenhouse. I hear it's gigundoly cool, like a rain forest or something."

We laughed. "Go ahead," I told Karen. "I'll come and find you in a little while. I want to see the greenhouse, too."

By that time David Michael had come back with the rakes, and he started to work next to Matt, who gestured to show him which section of the lawn and gardens they were working on.

Before I began raking, I asked Jessi to show me around a little. A few groups of BSC members and kids had already been hard at work that week, and I was curious about what they'd been doing.

"See this stone wall?" asked Jessi, as we began to tour the grounds. "It was starting to fall down, but Dawn came here with the Hobart boys, and they fixed it up."

"It looks great," I said.

"And this section here," Jessi said, showing me a path between two garden beds, "was overgrown with these viney weeds. Stacey and Charlotte Johanssen pulled them out and carted them away."

"Wow!" I said. By this time we'd moved far away from David Michael and Matt. I could barely hear the sound of their rakes.

"Kristy," whispered Jessi, "I have to tell you something." She looked around, as if to see whether anyone had followed us. Then she pulled me over to a stone garden bench, and we sat down.

"What is it?" I said. "You look upset."

"I am, a little," Jessi confessed. "It's just that some weird things have been happening here while we've been working."

"Such as?" I asked. I couldn't imagine what she might be talking about.

"Well, such as a bucket disappearing," Jessi said. "I know, it sounds crazy. But the first day we came here to work it wasn't so cold out, so I was scrubbing down that statue in the fountain. The one you passed on your way to find me today? And I took a break to help Becca with something, and when I came back my bucket was gone."

"Jessi, I don't think — " I was about to say that bucket disappearances didn't exactly rate up there with bizarre happenings, but Jessi interrupted me.

"That's not all," she said. "There were also some footprints near the greenhouse on Tuesday. You know, the day it snowed? We didn't see anybody walking around, but the footprints — they were man-sized ones — just *appeared* in the middle of the afternoon. And right near them was a big pile of weeds that Stacey and Charlotte swore they had put in the brush pile."

"Anything else?" I asked. I still wasn't convinced.

"Well, when I was raking leaves out of that summer house on Wednesday, I found an empty pack of matches. And Mrs. Goldsmith told me that nobody has been in there in months."

"Hmm," I said. "When you put it all together, it does sound a little strange. But who would be hanging around here? And why?"

"I don't know," said Jessi. "But I have a feeling whoever it is doesn't like all the work we're doing."

"What do you mean?" I asked.

"Well, it just seems like someone is trying to ruin the work we're doing. Or make it harder for us to get it done, anyway."

"By doing things like stealing your bucket," I mused.

"Right."

"Okay," I said. "Well, I'm glad you let me know. I'll keep my eyes open. Now, shouldn't we start working?"

I spent the next hour or so carting away the piles of leaves that David Michael, Jessi, and Matt had raked up. It felt good to be moving around outdoors, even though it was a chilly, gray day. I enjoyed the feeling of using my muscles for the first time in a while, and I even started to work up a little sweat. I didn't notice anything strange happening.

Until, that is, I found the card.

It was a white business card, lying on the ground under a weeping willow tree. I went by it once with my garden cart, but the next time I passed it I bent to pick it up. "DT DEVELOPERS," the card read. "Fine Quality Homes and Construction."

"DT Developers!" I said out loud. "Those must be the guys who want to buy this place." I thought for a second, and then it all became crystal clear. Everything Jessi had told me fell into place. Naturally the developers wouldn't want the arboretum cleaned up. They *liked* the fact that it looked terrible. For one thing, it might mean that nobody else — such as Mrs. VanderBellen — would want it. And for another thing, it would probably mean they could buy it for an even cheaper price.

"Sabotage!" I whispered under my breath. I felt a chill, and it had nothing to do with the weather.

# CHAPTER 8

"Lemon? Or milk?"

I stared down at the fragile teacup in front of me. It was decorated with pink roses and gold swirls, so delicate I was afraid it might break if I *looked* at it the wrong way. "Um, milk, please," I answered, finally, trying to sound sure of myself. I held out my cup, and Mrs. Abbott — Mrs. *Mildred* Abbott, great-grandniece of Christina Thomas — added milk to the tea she'd already poured from a silver teapot.

"Sugar?" she asked.

"Please," I answered. I watched with fascination as Mrs. Abbott used a pair of silver tongs to drop one lump of sugar into my cup.

"Another lump?"

"No, thank you," I said. "One is fine. Thank you."

As you can tell by all the pleases and thank yous, I was on my best behavior, and trying

70

hard to mind my manners. Mrs. Abbott, it turned out, was very much as I'd imagined her to be, but not entirely.

I knew from my research that Mrs. Abbott was about the same age as Nannie, but at first it seemed as if she and my grandmother were as different as night and day. Nannie dresses very casually, even when she has company. Mrs. Abbott was wearing a pretty green-and-white striped dress that looked as if it had been starched. (I sure was glad I'd worn my skirt!) Nannie loves to watch the Knicks play basketball. I had the feeling Mrs. Abbott wouldn't know a hoop if she were dunked through it. Nannie has been mentioned in the *Stoneybrook News* as one of the town's best senior bowlers. Mrs. Abbott probably wouldn't have been caught dead in bowling shoes.

Mrs. Abbott lived in an apartment near downtown Stoneybrook. It was the nicest, most elegant apartment I'd ever seen, with gorgeous Oriental rugs on the floors, and paintings in gold frames on all the walls. She was tall and thin, with perfectly white hair that was perfectly arranged. Her face was stern, and while her blue eyes were piercing — here's where I found the first surprise — they danced when she smiled. And she smiled (my second surprise) fairly often. Mrs. Abbott looked stern, but she really wasn't. She was funny, and interesting, and *interested*: in me (and in the BSC), and in my questions about Christina Thomas. My nervousness had pretty much disappeared about two seconds after we'd met.

The subject of the BSC came up when she asked me to tell her about myself. This was after my second lemon bar, but before my first piece of poppy-seed cake. (Another thing I learned about Mrs. Abbott is that she doesn't kid around when she invites someone to tea. And she is a terrific baker.)

I explained a little about the BSC. She nodded and smiled. "I've heard of your club," she said. "It sounds just wonderful. You and your friends must be very resourceful young women."

"Thank you," I said. (I was tired of those two words, but I couldn't think of anything else to say.) I figured she must have read about us in the paper, or seen one of our fliers. Most people in Stoneybrook have at least heard of the BSC, even if they're not clients.

"Another lemon bar?" she asked, passing the plate with a smile that told me she was keeping track of how many I'd had, and was pleased that I liked them.

"Thank you," I said, taking one. (Now I was *really* tired of those words.) I wanted to start asking her about Christina, but I wasn't sure how to begin.

"Now, about Christina," Mrs. Abbott said suddenly, as if she had read my mind. She settled back into her wing chair and folded her hands in her lap. She gave me that piercing gaze. "Where did you say you first found out about her?"

"In a book," I said. I told her about that day in Watson's study. "Her name caught my eye because it's so much like mine," I said.

Mrs. Abbott nodded. "Isn't that a coincidence?" she said. "Of course, Thomas is a fairly common name."

Suddenly I felt silly for having thought I might be *related* to Christina. Mrs. Abbott was right. Thomas *is* a common name. But it didn't matter. Something strange had happened to me in the last couple of days. The fact was, while I was doing my research in the library I'd realized something: the idea that I might have a fortune coming to me was less interesting than just finding out what had happened to Christina. I had begun to feel some connection to her, whether or not we were related, and — this may sound silly — I had also come to care about her. More than anything, I wanted to learn more about her mysterious story.

I didn't explain all of that to Mrs. Abbott. I just told her how Mary Anne, Claudia, and I had looked through the town records and old newspapers.

"My, you *have* been working hard, haven't you?" she asked, raising an eyebrow.

"Well, it's a fascinating story," I said.

"It is, isn't it?" Mrs. Abbott smiled and leaned forward. "Unfortunately, I seem to be the only one of her relatives who's interested in it. My cousin, Devon Thomas the fourth, used to be — but he's too busy now that his contracting business has gotten so big. I suspect I'm the only one who ever thinks about Christina anymore."

"*I've* been thinking about Christina," I said. "I can't stop thinking about her, as a matter of fact. Ever since I read about her disappearance — "

"Aah, the disappearance," said Mrs. Abbott. "Now that's a story."

"More like a mystery," I said. "I can't find out anything about where she went, or why. Except for one suggestion that she might have gone to Pennsylvania."

Mrs. Abbott nodded. "There were rumors about that," she said. "But the family squelched them. Her brother didn't want anyone to guess at the truth."

"The truth?" I asked. Suddenly I felt my

74

heart skip a beat. "Do you know the truth?"

"I do," she said. "Or, at least, I know as much of it as anyone does. Christina took *some* secrets to the grave with her." Mrs. Abbott's eyes were doing that dancing thing as she looked over at me. I knew she could tell how excited I was at the thought of learning more about Christina.

"Will you tell me what you know?" I asked.

"Of course I will. Why else would I have asked you here today?" She settled back into her chair and smoothed her dress. Then she began to tell Christina's story, which, she explained, she'd pieced together from entries in a diary she'd discovered.

"As you know, Christina's parents died when she was only sixteen. I've always thought it must have been quite a blow for her, especially since she was the only daughter. Most women in those days didn't have much say in the direction their lives took, you know." She looked at me sharply, and I nodded. "Even though she was the eldest child in that family, Christina was a girl. According to society's rules, that meant she had to listen to her brothers and do what they told her to do. She couldn't even do what she wanted with her inheritance!"

"That's no fair," I said. "I wouldn't have put up with it."

"Hmm," said Mrs. Abbott softly. "Maybe you are related to her." She looked intently at me, and then gave her head a little shake and continued the story. "It gets worse," she said. "You see, her brother Devon — that's Devon the first, of course — had a business partner by the name of Simon Clock. Simon was also Devon's best friend. The two of them hatched a plot together. Even though Christina had little or no romantic interest in Simon, Devon planned to force her to marry him. At that point, her inheritance would become Simon's, and he would invest it in the business he shared with Devon. They seemed to think it worked out well for everyone."

I was shaking my head. "What about Christina?" I asked. "What about her feelings? Did she love Simon?"

Mrs. Abbott frowned. "Hardly," she said. "Christina was in love with a young Union soldier — this was during the time of the Civil War, of course — named Henry Gordon. They planned to elope, but before they could, he was shipped out to Pennsylvania."

"Pennsylvania!" I said.

"That's right," said Mrs. Abbott. "And she may have ended up there. But we'll never know for sure."

"What do you mean?" I asked, almost jumping out of my chair. "Don't you know?" I didn't mean to be rude, but I couldn't believe the story was going to end here.

Mrs. Abbott didn't seem to notice how quickly I'd lost my manners. Instead, she picked up a leather-bound scrapbook that sat on a side table and pulled out a laminated page. "This is the last anyone ever heard of Christina," she said. "It's a letter she sent to Henry." She passed the letter to me, and I looked at it carefully.

The letter, which was in a beautiful script Mrs. Abbott told me was called "copperplate," went like this:

*Dear Henry,*

*I cannot marry Simon. I shall be your wife — or no one's. I must leave Stoneybrooke today. I shall come to look for you in Pennsylvania. If for any reason I do not find my way to you, I ask you only this: Look in our special place, on this day, at ten o'clock p.m.*

*Christina*

At the bottom was a date: February 14, 1863. The date was surrounded by a perfect circle, and around the circle, roses were drawn. Their twining stems were black, like the ink on the rest of the page, but their petals were painted brown.

"Whoa!" I said. I let out a big sigh as I

handed the letter back to Mrs. Abbott. "So she married Henry after all."

"I'm afraid not," said Mrs. Abbott, with a sad shake of her head. "This letter was returned to Devon by Henry's family. He was killed in battle before Christina arrived in Pennsylvania."

I gasped.

"His family thought the letter might lend a clue to Christina's disappearance, which they had been sorry to hear of. They had approved of their son's choice." Mrs. Abbott sighed. "But Devon never tried to find her. He was furious with her for humiliating him by refusing to marry his friend, and stated publicly that he was glad to be rid of her."

"But what about her fortune?" I asked. My head was spinning, but I hadn't forgotten that Christina's fortune had disappeared when she did.

"I've always believed that this letter holds a clue to its whereabouts," said Mrs. Abbott. "But I'm no detective, so I haven't been able to prove it."

Before I could stop to think, the words were out of my mouth. "Mrs. Abbott?" I asked. "Would you — would you let me make a copy of that letter? More than anything, I would love to help you solve this mystery."

She gave me that piercing look again. Then

her eyes began to dance. "Kristy Thomas," she said. "I have a feeling about you. Solving this mystery won't be easy, but if anyone can do it, I think you can. There's a copy shop across the street." She handed me the letter and I took it, but for a second I was so shocked I couldn't move. "Go on, girl," she said. "If you're quick about it, we'll have time for one more cup of tea when you get back."

That was all the encouragement I needed. I did as she'd told me, and an hour later I was on my way to our BSC meeting, clutching the copied letter in my hand.

# CHAPTER 9

Friday

Well, at least the greenhouse is still standing.... (That's supposed to be a joke! Ha-ha.) Silly me. I should have realized that Jackie Rodowsky + arboretum would = destruction. Fortunately, as Mrs. Goldsmith pointed out, nothing there is breakable or even that fragile (except for the greenhouse). And at least we did finally find his tooth — but I'm getting ahead of myself....

That entry in the club notebook was written by Mallory, after a long afternoon at the arboretum. ("Long?" she said later. "It seemed *endless!*")

Mal had thought the afternoon would be a lot of fun. She had a sitting job with one of our regular charges, Jackie Rodowsky (he's seven), and both Jessi and Mary Anne were sitting, too. The three of them decided ahead of time to take their charges to the arboretum.

"We'll only have a couple of hours, between school and our BSC meeting, but I bet we can get *tons* of work done with all those kids there," Jessi had said when they were planning their day. But, as Mal told me later, there was one thing they'd all forgotten: Jackie's nickname.

We love Jackie. He's a spunky little kid, with red hair and red cheeks (covered with freckles) to match. He's friendly and fun and outgoing. He also happens to be just about the most accident-prone kid any of us has ever met.

That's why we call him the Walking Disaster.

We don't call him that to his face, and we don't mean it in a bad way. As I said, we love Jackie. But it's important to remember that when Jackie's around, things are . . . well, never dull.

Mal remembered it that day as soon as she reached the Rodowskys' house. He must have been watching for her, because he appeared the moment she arrived. He ran out the front door, tripped and started to stumble, caught himself, tripped again, grabbed on to the porch railing (nearly pulling it out of its foundation), and fell anyway, into some bushes.

"Oh, Jackie," said Mal with a sigh. She could see that he was fine, since he was back on his feet and grinning within seconds.

"Hi, Mallory," said Jackie, waving. Then he stopped grinning and put his hand up to his mouth. "Uh-oh," he said.

"What?" asked Mal. "Are you all right?"

"Oh, I'm fine," said Jackie. "It's just that I had this tooth that was a little loose. Now it's even looser. I bet anything it comes out today!" He put his finger on the tooth and wiggled it.

"Great," said Mal. "Make sure you save it when it does, so you can put it under your pillow for the Tooth Fairy."

"I know *that*," said Jackie. "I've already lost lots of teeth."

(As Mal was telling me this part of the story, I began to feel a little queasy. There's something about teeth falling out that really bugs me. Mal's used to it, with all those younger brothers and sisters. But I can't stand seeing wiggly loose teeth. Ew. It's a good thing I was busy having tea with Mildred Abbott that day.)

By the time Mal and Jackie arrived at the arboretum, Jessi and Mary Anne were already there, along with their charges. Mary Anne was sitting for Marilyn and Carolyn Arnold, who are eight-year-old identical twins. None of us in the BSC has any trouble telling them apart, especially since Carolyn had her hair cut in a trendy style, but they do look an awful lot alike. They have very different interests, though. For example, that day Carolyn, who's interested in science, had decided she wanted to work with Mrs. Goldsmith in the greenhouse. Marilyn, the more outgoing twin, would be helping the "outdoor crew" with clearing brush and picking up litter, the two tasks Jessi had planned for the day.

Buddy and Suzi Barrett, Jessi's charges, were eager to start work. Suzi's five, and she wanted to work in the greenhouse "with all the pretty flowers." Buddy, who's eight, was set to work outside. "I've been helping Franklin work in our new yard," he explained proudly. "I know how to do lots of stuff now."

Franklin is Buddy's stepfather, Franklin DeWitt. He and Mrs. Barrett got married recently. In fact, they were married in Stoneybrook on the same weekend Dawn's dad was married in California. The DeWitt-Barrett marriage is one the BSC looked forward to for a long time. We always thought that when Mr. DeWitt, who has four children, married Mrs. Barrett, who has three (Buddy and Suzi have a little sister named Marnie), it would be like Stoneybrook's version of the Brady Bunch. And it is, sort of. Let's just say that the two families are still adjusting to each other.

That day, the DeWitt kids had gone to visit their grandmother, and Mrs. Barrett had taken Marnie shopping with her, Jessi was sitting just for Buddy and Suzi. Which, she told Mal, was fine with her. Sitting for the entire Barrett-DeWitt clan is a *major* job these days.

As soon as Jackie saw the other kids that day, he ran to show them his loose tooth. Mal joined Mary Anne and Jessi, and the three of them talked about the plan for the afternoon.

"I spoke to Mrs. Goldsmith already," Jessi told them, "and I have a plan figured out. The kids are all set to work, too. The only thing I didn't tell them — " (she glanced at the group of kids to make sure they weren't listening) " — is that I'm going to be keeping my eyes peeled for signs of sabotage. I don't want to get the kids all worried about it, but Kristy and I are pretty sure there's something going on here. So let me know if you see anything strange."

Mary Anne and Mal nodded. Then Jessi called the kids over. "Okay, Suzi and Carolyn, Mrs. Goldsmith is waiting for you in the greenhouse," she said. "You others, grab a rake and a garbage bag and follow me!"

Mal offered to show Suzi and Carolyn to the greenhouse. And by the time she came back to find him, Jackie had already had his first minor accident.

"It wasn't my fault!" he was saying, when she found him sprawled on the ground, next to an empty concrete pedestal. Nearby was the large, round, dish-shaped birdbath that had, a second ago, been sitting on top of the pedestal. "All I did was run by it," said Jackie. "It must not have been on there right, because I didn't even touch it. Really!" He put his finger to his mouth, to see if his loose tooth was still there.

"It's okay," said Mal. She checked the birdbath for cracks, but it was still in one piece. "Help me lift it back on, okay?" She bent down and grabbed the dish. "One, two, three, *heave*!" They picked up the birdbath and set it on top of its stand. Mal stood back to look at it, and then moved forward again to adjust it slightly. "It feels solid now," she said. Later, she told me she wondered about that birdbath. Had somebody purposely set it slightly askew, so it would fall — and maybe break?

Meanwhile, Mary Anne and Jessi were finding something else suspicious. When Mal and Jackie caught up with them, they were standing near an area of the grounds that looked as if it needed some serious raking.

"What are we waiting for?" asked Jackie, picking up a rake. "Let's start." He and Buddy and Marilyn began to rake, pushing dead grass and leaves into a big pile.

Jessi just stood there, staring at the ground.

"What's the matter?" Mary Anne asked her.

Jessi shook her head. "I must be going nuts," she said. "I could have sworn we raked this exact place yesterday. I mean, it was raked *clean*. And now look at it."

Mal looked around. "I see a tarp over there, draped on those bushes," she said. "Were you using that?"

Jessi nodded. "We left it over the last pile of stuff we raked," she answered. "We were going to drag it to the compost area today."

"Well, there's your answer," said Mary Anne. "The tarp must have blown off the pile, and then the wind blew the leaves and trash around. What a shame!"

"It's a shame all right," said Mal quietly. "But I'm not so sure the wind is responsible, if you know what I mean." She shook her head. "I really think somebody is out to make this place look bad," she finished.

And during the rest of the afternoon, Mal kept finding what she was sure was evidence that someone was sabotaging the arboretum. She also stayed busy chasing after Jackie, who was involved in one mess after another.

First, he danced around in an empty fountain, pretending he was one of the cherub statues, until he almost knocked one of them over. That was when he found the empty potato chip bags that Mal was sure must have been thrown there on purpose. Next, Jackie pulled out about twenty plant markers, "because they're all rusty." Mal and Jessi had to put each one back, relying on Jessi's memory (Mrs. Goldsmith had given her a very complete tour of the gardens before she started working) and on a plant-identification book Mrs. Goldsmith had lent them. While they were doing that, they found more evidence that pointed to sabotage: footprints, knocked-over flowerpots, and a newly broken trellis.

Finally, at the end of the day, Jackie ran to Mal, who was trying to fix the trellis.

"My tooth!" Jackie cried.

"Did it finally come out?" Mal asked. "Great!"

"Not great," said Jackie. "I can't find it anywhere. And I *have* to have it. Otherwise the Tooth Fairy won't leave me anything."

That was the end of work for *that* day. The

whole crew ended up searching every area they'd worked in, looking for Jackie's tooth. The kids made a game of it and had a great time, but Mal, Jessi, and Mary Anne couldn't get their minds off the evidence they'd found. They were convinced that somebody was trying to undo all the work they were doing. Things didn't look good for the arboretum.

Oh — the tooth? As Mal told me later, Jackie was the one who finally found it. It had fallen into his shirt pocket.

"I had to laugh," she said. "After a day like that, there's nothing else you can do. Unless you want to cry!"

# CHAPTER 10

$G$uess who broke the "club business first" rule at Friday's BSC meeting?

We all did.

I did it first, though. There was no way I could wait to spill the big news about my tea with Mildred Abbott — and show my friends the letter I'd copied. After that, Jessi, Mal, and Mary Anne brought up their news, about the evidence they'd found at the arboretum.

I may be wrong, but I don't ever remember a club meeting where less club business was discussed. Oh, we answered a few phone calls, and arranged some jobs, but other than that we didn't discuss a thing but the two big mysteries we had found ourselves involved in.

And we spent most of our time talking about the letter from Christina.

Mary Anne (naturally) thought it was the most romantic letter she'd ever seen. She read it over and over again, sighing and wiping away an occasional tear.

Claudia just loved the mystery of the story. She had that Nancy Drew gleam in her eyes as she speculated about what had happened to Christina and her fortune. "The question is," she said, "how do we trace things from here?"

Stacey and Dawn were both interested in the fact that the letter said Henry should look in "our special place."

"Look for what?" asked Stacey. "Do you think the fortune is hidden there?"

"If we could only find the special place, I bet we could solve the mystery," said Dawn. "That's the key. The special place."

Mal liked the roses Christina had drawn on the letter. "She was a good artist," she said admiringly. "I like the way their stems twine around."

Jessi agreed. "They look real," she said.

We talked about the letter all through Friday's BSC meeting. We talked about it — over the phone and during our work at the arboretum — over the weekend. And we were still talking about it at school on Monday morning, while I rummaged through my locker trying to find my math notebook.

Dawn, Claudia, and Mary Anne were clustered around my locker, and Dawn was telling us she'd had a dream about Christina the night before. "I *saw* her," she said, her eyes round. (Dawn loves ghost stories, and I could tell Christina's story reminded her of one.) "She was walking down the road, carrying a suitcase."

"Leaving Stoneybrook," Mary Anne said. "To find Henry." She sighed, and her eyes got all misty.

"And to escape Simon," Claudia reminded her. "She left Stoneybrook, and everything familiar, and probably her *fortune* behind, because she didn't believe her brother should force her to marry somebody she didn't love."

"She was no pushover," said Dawn. "It must have been hard to be a strong, determined woman in those days."

"Hey, it's not so easy even now," I said. "But we Thomas women have always worked at it!" I grinned at my friends. Then I looked over Dawn's shoulder and saw something that made me frown. "Check it out," I said, nudging Mary Anne, who turned to see what — or should I say *who* — I was looking at.

"Ugh," said Mary Anne. "Why is Cokie lurking around?"

Cokie Mason is one of the BSC's favorite people. *Not.* She's never been someone I would call a friend, even though I've known her for years. Cokie is just one of those people who are out for themselves. She has stooped to some pretty low tricks to get what she wants, whether that's making the BSC look bad or stealing other girls' boyfriends.

Believe it or not, Cokie even tried to steal Logan away from Mary Anne! (Anybody who would do something mean to a sweet person like Mary Anne has to be the lowest of the low, in my book.) If you asked her about it, she'd tell you she was only dating Logan to keep him company during a time when he and Mary Anne had temporarily broken up. But the truth is that Cokie's always had a crush on Logan, and she moved in on him like a shark the minute she thought Mary Anne was out of the picture.

Mary Anne once referred to Cokie as her "mortal enemy."

"Just ignore her," I said.

"I bet she's trying to figure out if she can get Logan in her clutches again," said Mary Anne. She looked worried. "That must be why she's hanging around as if she's spying on us."

I shot a Look at Cokie, trying to scare her off. Then I turned back to Mary Anne. "Don't worry," I said, in a voice I hoped would carry. "Logan couldn't be less interested in her." I gave up on finding my math notebook and slammed my locker door. "By the way, I won't be at the arboretum this afternoon," I announced to my friends. "I'm going to the library, to do some more research on Christina. I want to find out where the family's home, Squirelot, was. If I can find that, maybe I can find the special place she talks about in her letter."

"Good luck," said Mary Anne. "If you figure anything out, you can tell us about it at the BSC meeting."

After school that day, I headed over to the library. I could have taken a bus there, but I decided to walk, since it was actually a pretty nice day. I guess we were having the February version of a January thaw. The sun had been out all day and the last of the grimy snow had finally melted. I took deep breaths as I walked along, enjoying the way the soft, warm air smelled. It smelled like dirt, which might not sound so great. But after a long winter, I happen to think the smell of fresh earth is wonderful. It was making me remember how beautiful Watson's flower gardens look in the middle of June. I thought of the arboretum, and wondered what it would look like in the middle of June — that is, if it wasn't being bulldozed for a development.

I felt a little guilty about not working at the

arboretum that day. There wasn't much time left to prepare it to be seen by that wealthy donor who was thinking about buying it. (According to Mrs. Goldsmith, Mrs. VanderBellen would be coming by sometime that week.) But I also felt tied up in the Christina mystery. It was as if I were being *pulled* toward the library that day. I *had* to keep trying to solve the mystery of Christina's missing fortune.

I felt so energized by my walk that when I arrived at the library I took the steps two at a time. Inside, I headed straight for the reference room, waving and smiling at Mrs. Kishi as I passed by her office. The smile was still on my face when I turned the corner into the area where the microfilm machines sit. But then I saw Cokie Mason, and my smile disappeared.

"Hi, Kristy," said Cokie.

"Hi," I said. "What are you doing here?" As far as I know, Cokie never does extra schoolwork if she can help it. It was just my luck to run into her at the library.

"Waiting for a friend," said Cokie. "Actually, I was on my way out."

I watched her leave, but I didn't see her meet any friend. I figured she must be seeing some boy her parents didn't approve of.

I turned my attention away from Cokie and toward the microfilm machine. What was it I needed to look for? I tried to remember what Claudia had told me. Then I snapped my fingers. She'd mentioned some town records that might help me out, and she'd told me where to find them. I headed for the drawer.

When I pulled it out, it felt light. And as soon as I looked into it, I saw why. It was nearly empty. I checked the remaining reels, but they weren't ones I needed. Every single one I wanted to look at was missing!

I looked around the reference room, hoping to figure out who had the reels. Both microfilm readers were free, so nobody was using the reels that minute. There were several people sitting at the work tables: two high school girls, a nurse dressed in her uniform, and a man wearing a fairly dirty pair of overalls. None of them seemed to have the microfilm, though.

"Can I help you?"

One of the library aides was behind me. He must have noticed how lost I looked. "Well, I — I was trying to find some microfilm," I said. "But it's not in its drawer."

"Well, it can't be checked out, since it's reference material," said the aide. "But it's probably in that bin over there, waiting to be reshelved." He sighed. "We're way behind today, so I doubt I can get it processed for you right away. Can you come back tomorrow? Or is there something else I can help you find?"

"Well," I said, "I was hoping to find out more about this old estate called Squirelot. It used to belong to a family named Thomas, and it was here in Stoneybrook. But I don't know *where* it was. Is there any way to figure that out?"

"Let's see," said the aide. He frowned and stroked his chin. Then his eyes lit up. "I know!" he said. "We have a book about the history of Stoneybrook. I think it has some old maps in it." He led me to the local history area and ran his finger along a shelf of books. "Here it is," he said, pulling one out. "If you'll check the index, I think you might find what you're looking for."

"Thanks!" I said. "Thanks a lot." As I walked back to the work table, I opened the book and started to leaf through it. I've looked at a lot of books about Stoneybrook history, but this was one I'd never seen before. It was full of old maps. I started to feel excited. If only I could find Squirelot. I was ready to bet that Christina's fortune was hidden on its grounds.

I turned to the index and found several listings for maps of Stoneybrook in the mid-1800s. "Page one-sixty-eight," I muttered, turning back to check the page that seemed most likely. And as soon as I found it, I saw something that made me blink. Sure enough, on the map on page 168 there was a large area marked off with "Squirelot" written across it.

And Squirelot had been circled — in red ink.

"That's strange," I said under my breath. Then I looked back at the map. I still couldn't tell where Squirelot was in relation to modern Stoneybrook — although something about its placement seemed familiar. What I had to do next was figure out how the old map would compare to a new one. I carried the book to a Stoneybrook map that's posted on the reference room wall.

It didn't take long to find some common landmarks: an old church, a little park, a cemetery. I looked up at the present-day map and then glanced down at the book in my hands. Back and forth, back and forth. And then, suddenly, it was as if a lightbulb clicked on in my brain. "Of course!" I said, so loudly that everyone else in the room looked at me. I was so amazed by my discovery that I just smiled back at them. I didn't care if they thought I was crazy. What I had just discovered had put me one big step forward on the path to solving Christina's mystery.

# CHAPTER 11

Monday
Talk about uncovering a secret! I can't believe we didn't figure out the truth about the arboretum before now! The big question is, what do we do next?

"Sabotage? What does that mean?"

Dawn and Jessi whirled around. "Charlotte!" said Dawn.

"Becca!" said Jessi. "How long have you guys been standing there?"

"Long enough to hear what you were talking about," said Becca. "And we want to know what's going on." She folded her arms across her chest and raised her eyebrows, waiting to hear what Dawn and Jessi had to say.

It was Monday, the same afternoon I'd spent at the library. Dawn was sitting for Charlotte Johanssen, and they had joined Jessi and Becca at the arboretum. After helping Becca and Charlotte start in on the job of clearing leaves out of a flower bed, Jessi had pulled Dawn aside for a serious talk. "Keep your eyes open," Jessi had said. "We really think someone may be out to ruin Mrs. Goldsmith's plans for the arboretum. We may not be able to catch the people who are doing it, but at least we can try to fix up whatever they mess up. We can't let the sabotage work."

That was when Charlotte and Becca interrupted.

"We weren't eavesdropping," Becca explained, when Jessi glared at her. "We just came to ask you where the extra wheelbarrow is. And we couldn't help hearing what you said."

"If something's wrong, we want to help," said Charlotte. "I thought we were helping to save the arboretum. Is it in even more trouble?"

Jessi and Dawn exchanged glances. Then Jessi shrugged. "I guess we might as well tell them," she said to Dawn. "It can't hurt."

Jessi led the others over to a couple of garden benches near the fountain. "It's like this," she told Charlotte and Becca, when they were all seated. "You know how we're cleaning up this place so that a rich lady might buy it and keep it running?" The girls nodded. "Well," Jessi continued, "there are some *other* people who want to tear down the arboretum and build houses here. They're called developers."

"But Mrs. Goldsmith wouldn't want that to happen!" said Becca.

"Right," said Jessi. "Neither would we. This is a really special place, and it's part of Stoneybrook's history. But if the lady doesn't want to buy it, the developers probably will."

"What about that sabo — whatever?" asked Charlotte.

"Sabotage," said Dawn. "It means when somebody wrecks the work that somebody else is doing, on purpose."

"And we think that may be what's happen-

ing here," said Jessi. "We think somebody —
maybe a developer is messing up the arboretum as fast as we're cleaning it up, so
that when the lady comes she won't be impressed."

"So she won't buy the place," said Becca,
nodding.

"And *they* can buy it, and tear it all down
for houses," added Charlotte. "That's terrible!"

"We don't have proof," Jessi reminded the
girls. "So far there are just some clues, but we
haven't been able to put them all together."

"Clues? Maybe we can help!" said Charlotte. "I've helped solve mysteries before, you
know."

Jessi and Dawn looked at each other and
grinned. It was true. Charlotte is a good detective, and she's been helpful in unraveling
more than one of the mysteries the BSC has
been involved in.

"I think *I* know a clue," said Becca.

"You do?" asked Jessi, turning to look at
her.

Becca nodded. "One day last week I was
working with Mrs. Goldsmith in the greenhouse. I looked out the window and saw these
two men in overalls, way over by where the
apple trees are."

"What were they doing?" asked Dawn.

101

"They were just walking around," said Becca. "And they had these things they would set up and look through, like they were taking pictures. Only they weren't."

"How do you know?" asked Jessi.

"Mrs. Goldsmith said so," explained Becca. "When I told her about the men, she looked at them and said they were probably — I forget the word. People who measure land. She thought it was strange that they were there, because she hadn't asked them to come. She seemed a little bit upset."

"Hmmm, very interesting," said Jessi. "I'll bet it was surveyors you saw." Becca nodded, and Jessi went on. "I wonder if the developers sent them," she mused.

"Maybe. But we can't prove it," Dawn reminded her.

"Still, I'm glad you told us, Becca," said Jessi. "Anyway, as I was just saying to Dawn, I think the best thing to do is keep our eyes open. It almost doesn't matter whether or not we prove that the developers are sabotaging our work. The main thing is to make sure the arboretum looks great. So if we find any messes, we have to clean them up right away."

"We can do that," said Becca earnestly.

"No problem," said Charlotte. "But while I'm cleaning up, I'm also going to be watching

102

for clues. If somebody's doing something wrong, I want to catch them and make sure they stop."

Charlotte has a very firm sense of right and wrong.

"Okay, then," said Jessi, standing up and smacking her hands together. "Let's get back to work. I'll help you guys find that wheel-barrow."

"And I'll start clearing those vines off the house," said Dawn, looking up at the long brick wall of the main building. It was covered with old, dead vines, and Mrs. Goldsmith had told Jessi that they needed to be pulled down before they ruined the bricks.

"Don't forget to wear the gloves Mrs. Gold-smith loaned me," Jessi told her.

Dawn thanked Jessi for the reminder, pulled on the gloves, and started in on the vines as Jessi and the girls headed off to find the wheel-barrow. Those vines were clinging pretty tightly to the wall, Dawn told me later. "I could see what Mrs. Goldsmith meant about their ruining the brick," she said.

Dawn pulled and tugged at the vines, mak-ing big piles of the ones she'd pulled down. The vines were so entwined, and they climbed so far up the building, that Dawn thought they must have been growing there for years and years. Slowly, she worked her way from one end of the building to the other. When Jessi came back from helping the girls, she started pulling vines down, too. She worked on another wall, around the corner from Dawn's.

"This is hard work!" Jessi called, stopping to wipe her forehead.

"I know!" Dawn called back. "I can't believe I'm almost finished with this side."

There was silence for a few minutes. Then Jessi heard a yelp. "Dawn?" she called. "What happened?"

There was no answer, so Jessi headed around the corner to see if Dawn was all right. "Dawn?" she asked again, when she saw a white-faced Dawn staring at part of the wall she'd just cleared.

"Come here," Dawn said to Jessi in a strange voice.

Jessi stepped closer and looked up. "Wow!" she said. "A brass plaque. Neat! It must tell something about the building."

"It does," said Dawn in the same strange voice. "Read it."

Jessi stepped closer and read the plaque. "Whoa!" she breathed, when she saw what it said. Then she and Dawn read it out loud together.

"Do you realize what this *means*?" Dawn asked, reaching out to run her fingers over the raised letters on the plaque.

"This is awesome!" Jessi said.

"What's awesome?"

Once again, Jessi and Dawn whirled around. And once again, Charlotte and Becca stood staring at them. "We could hear you all the way over by our flower bed," Becca explained.

"Is this another mystery?" asked Charlotte.

"It is," said Dawn, giving in to her excitement. "And it's a good one, too. Want to hear about it?" There was no way any more work was going to get done that afternoon. Dawn and Jessi took the girls to the garden benches again, sat them down, and filled them in on what they'd found out and what it could mean.

After that, Dawn and Jessi and the girls scoured the arboretum, looking for more clues. They turned over flowerpots, peeked inside birdhouses, and ran their hands over brick walls, searching for secret hiding places. Dawn looked closely at some of the fancy carvings on the wooden porch railings, wondering if one of the beautifully formed flowers or trees might actually be a secret button she could push to open a hidden wall. They poked into the underbrush and examined the pipes going into the fountain. Becca even began to dig in one of the gardens, insisting that a mound near the lily beds looked suspicious, until

Dawn put a stop to her excavations.

"We can't tear the place apart," Dawn said, looking around at the mess they'd made. "We're trying to neaten it up, remember?"

"You're right," said Jessi. "We need to make a better plan for searching." She paused and glanced at her watch. "But we'll have to clean up tomorrow. Right now, we have a BSC meeting to get to."

Dawn smiled. "No way do I want to be late to *that*. I can't wait to see Kristy's face when she hears what we found out," she said. "Will she be shocked, or what?"

# CHAPTER 12

Well, as you might have guessed by now, the answer to Dawn's question was "or what." I *wasn't* shocked — because what the brass plaque said and what I found in the book of old maps made the same thing clear.

The arboretum was Squirelot, and Squirelot was the arboretum.

Not surprisingly, the scene at our BSC meeting that Monday afternoon was total chaos. Picture this: Dawn and Jessi are babbling about a brass plaque, while Mal and Claudia yell questions at them a mile a minute. Stacey is trying to tell everybody she has to collect dues, but nobody can hear her over the racket. The phone is ringing off the hook. Mary Anne has her hands over her ears, and she's begging everybody to just "Slow down, *please*! And take turns!"

And me? Madame president? Did I stay out of the mess and maintain some dignity? No way. I was right in there, yelling *my* head off about maps and landmarks. The rule about BSC business always coming first was out the window. This was no ordinary meeting. Oh, we answered the phone when it rang, and assigned jobs, but that was about it. That day, the mystery came first.

Eventually we calmed down a bit and started to sort out what we'd learned. I explained about using the maps at the library to figure out where Squirelot had been. "I couldn't believe my eyes at first," I said. "But by the time I had double- and triple-checked the old map against the newer one, I knew it had to be true."

"And now there's *really* no question," Dawn said. "That plaque we found makes it definite."

"What did it say, exactly?" asked Mal.

Jessi reached into her backpack and pulled out a little notebook. "I wrote it down," she said. Then she read out loud: "Squirelot. Donated by Ellen, Scott, and Mary Thomas in memory of their grandparents, Rachel and John Thomas, and of their aunt, Christina Thomas." She looked up. "If I remember that family tree right, Scott and Mary Thomas were Edward's children."

"Wow! So it really is true," Mary Anne said. "Dawn's right. The plaque proves it. I can just picture Christina at the arboretum, back when it was a fancy estate. Can't you see her, wandering through the gardens on a summer evening, dressed in a long white gown?"

"And looking for a spot to hide her fortune," added Claudia. "While Devon chases after her, trying to force her to marry his awful friend."

"I wonder if her fortune really is hidden on the grounds," Stacey said.

"I'll bet anything it is," said Dawn. "Where else would it be? In those days, women didn't go out alone too often. She wouldn't have had the chance to find a secret place anywhere else."

"A stash of gold," mused Mal. "Think of it, all that money just lying buried for all these years."

"It's probably worth even more now than when she hid it," I put in. "What if it's, like, a million dollars worth of gold?"

"A million dollars," breathed Claudia. She had this look in her eyes as she started to fantasize. "Think of all the art supplies that would buy. I could even build myself a studio."

"I'd go on a shopping spree," said Stacey. "In Paris." She smiled to herself.

"How much does a private jet cost?" Dawn asked. "If I had my own, I could fly back and forth between here and California as often as I liked."

"As long as we're dreaming," said Mal, "I think I'll buy a ranch out in Montana, with stables full of gorgeous horses."

"I'll come live there with you," said Jessi. "If you build me a ballet studio in one wing, that is."

"I'd be happy to," said Mal, grinning. "We'll put it right next to my writing studio."

"Let's see," I said. "I'll start with season tickets to the Mets. Box seats, of course. Then, I'll buy official uniforms and equipment for the Krushers. After that — " Suddenly, I stopped myself. "What am I saying?" I asked. "The first thing I'll do is save the arboretum. After all, the money belongs there, right?"

"Definitely," said Jessi. "I can't wait to see Mrs. Goldsmith's face when we tell her that she never has to worry again about the arboretum closing."

"So it's settled," said Stacey, who had a strange look on her face. "The money goes to the arboretum." Everybody nodded. Stacey looked around at us and shook her head. "Don't you realize that there's one tiny thing we're forgetting?" She paused. "All this fantasizing is fun, but come on, you guys, *we haven't found the money yet!*"

"Oh, that," said Claudia, waving a hand. "That's only a matter of time."

"Oh, really?" asked Stacey, arching an eye-

110

brow. "Well, we'd better start, then. What do we do first?"

I could tell Stacey thought she was humoring Claudia. But Claudia was dead serious. "Well," she said thoughtfully, "I guess the first thing to do would be to look at the clues we have so far. Let's put everything out on the desk here, where we can look it over." She rummaged around in a drawer and came up with the family tree we'd made. I added my copy of Christina's letter (which I'd been carrying around in my backpack), and Jessi tore a page out of her notebook — the one on which she'd written down what the plaque said — and handed it over.

We clustered around Claudia's desk and stared at the three pieces of paper.

"Not much to go on," Stacey said, after a few minutes.

"It isn't, is it?" asked Dawn. "But let's think. Kristy, Mrs. Abbott said she'd always thought that this letter held some clues, right?"

"Right," I said. "But if they're there, I can't make any sense of them."

"Well, it seems obvious to me that the letter was supposed to lead Henry to the hidden fortune," said Mary Anne, after she'd reread the letter carefully. "She must have loved him so much," she added with a sigh.

"Okay," I said. "Let's not get all sentimen-

tal. What can we figure out from the letter?"
I pointed to the date. "February fourteenth.
Why that date? Obviously it has some special
meaning."

"It's Valentine's Day," said Mary Anne,
sighing again.

"Maybe the fortune's hidden under that
statue of the people kissing," said Jessi. "Get
it? Romance — kissing — Valentine's Day?"

"I get it," said Claudia, "but I don't know.
It's a little far-fetched. Still, I guess we could
check there." She wrote down "check statue"
on the list she'd started. (Only she spelled it
"statchew.")

"Or maybe by one of the birdhouses?"
asked Mal. "You know, lovebirds?"

Claudia made a note. "It won't hurt to check
every place we can think of," she said. "A
good detective follows up every single lead."

"I've been thinking," said Stacey, who had
been quiet for a few minutes. "What about
those roses around the date? Christina obviously put some time into drawing them.
They're beautiful."

"They are," said Claudia. "But what are you
trying to say?"

"Isn't there a rose garden at the arboretum?"
asked Stacey.

Jessi jumped up. "There is!" she said. "It's
supposed to be gorgeous when it's in bloom.

It's right in back of the main house."

"Maybe the rose garden was Christina's and Henry's special place," said Stacey.

"Whoa!" I said. "I bet you're right." I glanced down at the letter again.

"But — I hate to say this — wouldn't the garden have changed since Christina's day?" asked Dawn.

"No!" said Jessi. "Mrs. Goldsmith told me that the rose garden has been kept in its original condition for over a hundred years."

"That's it, then," said Claudia, making one last note and pushing back her chair. "I think we should go to the arboretum right after school tomorrow and check out the roses."

The next day, we headed over to the arboretum as soon as school was out. Jessi went inside to check in with Mrs. Goldsmith while the rest of us walked around back.

"Oh, no," said Dawn, as soon as we turned the corner and saw the gardens. "I forgot about this mess we left yesterday. We'd better clean it up before we leave."

"We will," said Claudia impatiently. "But first we have some clues to follow up."

Jessi came out the back door just then and motioned for us to follow her to the rose garden. "Mrs. Goldsmith was a little upset about the mess back here," she said, as she led the way. "But I promised her we'd clean it up today. I didn't tell her anything about what we're up to."

"Good," I said. "That way we can surprise her when we find the fortune."

We followed Jessi through a trellised arch and into a little garden I'd never seen before. I tried to imagine how it would be when the roses were blooming, but it was hard. All I could see were brownish, dead-looking sticks poking up. Then I peered closer at one of the clusters. "Hey!" I said, bending down to the ground. "Somebody's been digging here."

My friends joined me. "Look at that," Dawn said, checking out the pile of earth that had been shoved aside. "Whoever it was gave up before they dug too deeply. The ground is muddy on top, but it must still be frozen underneath."

"Check it out!" said Stacey, pointing to a patch of ground a little way off. "Footprints. They're small ones, though. Like *our* size."

My heart was beating fast. I knew — I just knew — that we were on to something. Something important. "We're not the only ones hunting for that fortune," I said quietly, as I looked down at the footprints.

"But who else could possibly know about it?" asked Dawn.

114

"Becca and Charlotte," said Jessi. "Don't you think?" She looked around at the rest of us.

"I don't know what to think," said Claudia. "But, no matter what, we'd better work fast. Let's get some shovels and start digging!"

Half an hour later, we were scattered around the grounds of the arboretum. Claudia, Stacey, and I were digging (or trying to dig; the ground was still hard) in the rose garden.

Jessi and Mary Anne were checking out the area near the statue Jessi had wondered about, and Mal and Dawn were excavating underneath the birdhouse, just in case Mal's idea about lovebirds might be right. We hadn't even begun to clean up the mess from the day before, so the arboretum was looking as if an army had marched through it. We weren't thinking about that, though. We were too busy looking for the missing fortune. We were so busy, in fact, that we didn't even hear the sound of a car pulling into the driveway of the arboretum.

That was why it was a total surprise to look up from our treasure-hunting and see Mrs. Goldsmith staring at us — with Mrs. VanderBellen, decked out in a fancy red coat and high heels, standing beside her.

Neither of them looked very happy.

## CHAPTER 13

"Yes, I understand," I said into the phone, nodding as I spoke as if the person on the other end could see me. "Uh-huh. Right. Sure. Okay." I paused. "Can I just say one more time how sorry — oh. Right. Okay, then. Good-bye." I hung up and looked around the room. Six glum faces looked back at me. I hated having to tell them what that phone call had been about.

It was Wednesday afternoon, and we were in the middle of a BSC meeting. It had been a very subdued meeting, especially compared to the ones we'd been having lately. Nobody seemed to feel like talking about the mystery or about anything else. We felt horrible about what a mess we'd made of things at the arboretum. As Jessi pointed out, we had done the opposite of what we had set out to do there. Instead of sprucing up the place to make it look attractive, we had made it look worse than ever.

"That was Mrs. Goldsmith, wasn't it?" Jessi asked.

I had been stalling, hoping I wouldn't have to tell everyone the bad news. But I couldn't stall anymore. "Yes," I said.

"And?" asked Stacey. "What happened after we left yesterday?"

The day before, when Mrs. Goldsmith and Mrs. VanderBellen had surprised us, we had tried to apologize for the mess. But Mrs. Goldsmith had just shaken her head and asked us to leave. We took off as quickly as we could.

"Mrs. Goldsmith said that after we left. Mrs. VanderBellen took a quick look around, decided she wasn't interested in buying the arboretum after all, and said good-bye." I said that as fast as I could and then looked down at my hands. I didn't want to see my friends' faces. I knew they'd look as horrified and guilty as mine.

"Oh, no." I heard Mary Anne gasp. "How awful."

"I feel terrible," Claudia said. "How could we have gotten so carried away?" I looked up in time to see her stick her hand into a bag of M&Ms and pull out a handful. She stared down at them, and shook her head. "I don't think even chocolate is going to make me feel better," she said mournfully. She dumped the handful back into the bag.

"After all that time we spent worrying about somebody else sabotaging our work," said Jessi, who was sitting on the floor, cradling her chin in her hands, "we sabotaged ourselves. How am I ever going to make it up to Mrs. Goldsmith?"

"If we'd found the fortune," said Mal, "we could give her the money. But we didn't find a thing." She patted Jessi on the back. "Still, Mrs. Goldsmith will forgive us," she added. "Someday. Maybe."

"I can't believe we'll never find out where the fortune was," said Dawn. "Now it'll probably stay hidden for another hundred years."

"Maybe Christina would have wanted it that way," said Stacey. "After all, she left it for Henry, not for a bunch of baby-sitters." She shook back her hair and frowned.

I couldn't believe what I was hearing. I mean, I felt guilty about what had happened, too, but I wasn't about to let it stop me from solving the mystery of Christina's fortune. "Hold on a second!" I said. "Do you all *hear* yourselves?" I got up and started to pace around the room. "Don't tell me you're ready to give up."

"What else can we do?" asked Jessi. "Dig

up the rest of the arboretum? I doubt Mrs. Goldsmith would appreciate that."

"No," I said, "but she would appreciate having a share of that fortune." I sat down in the director's chair again and looked around at my friends' skeptical faces. "I'm serious, you guys. I was thinking about it last night, and I really believe we have to keep trying."

"Okay, fine," said Dawn. "Maybe you're right. But how? Obviously, the way we were going about it wasn't right. You can't just dig holes all over the place."

"Plus, we need to work fast," I said. "Remember, somebody else might be looking for that fortune, too. That's why I brought this." I rummaged around in my backpack and pulled out a heavy, leather-bound book. I held it up.

"What's that?" asked Stacey. "A treasure hunter's guide?"

"Very funny," I said. "No, it's *The Stoneybrooke Town Record*. The book where we first found a mention of Christina."

"What good is that going to do us?" asked Claudia. "You already checked all the stuff about the Thomas family in there, didn't you?"

I nodded. "Here's what I was thinking," I said. "Remember when we were trying to figure out what was important about February fourteenth? Well, the almanac section of this book can tell us all about February fourteenth, eighteen sixty-three. I grabbed it on my way over here, thinking maybe we'd find some clues if we looked through it."

"Hmm," said Claudia. Suddenly I saw a certain gleam come back into her eyes — the gleam that means she's on the case. I noticed the other members of the BSC perking up a little, too. "So, what does it say?" Claudia asked, reaching for a notebook and pen.

I opened the book and flipped through it, looking for the right page. "Here we go," I said, after I'd run my finger down the entries for February 1863. "First of all, it says there was a cow auction at the Gleeson farm."

"A cow auction. That's meaningful," Stacey muttered.

I shot her a Look.

"Forty-nine of the finest heifers were sold to bidders from three counties," I read, just to torture Stacey. "Sounds like a lot of fun."

"Right," said Stacey, grinning a little in spite of herself. "If you happen to like cows."

The atmosphere in Claudia's room had started to lighten, and I was glad. I can't stand to sit around feeling depressed or worried. Not if I can be *doing* something, instead. I smiled around at my friends. Then I looked back down at the book and read the next entry. "Hmm, that's interesting," I said.

"What?" asked Jessi eagerly. "What does it say?"

"It says that Mrs. Jacob Smythe, the baker's wife, has left her home and taken up residence with her sister, Mrs. Matthew Poole."

"What does that have to do with the missing fortune?" asked Mal.

"Nothing," I admitted. "But it makes good gossip, doesn't it? Don't you wonder why she left him, and if she ever went back? Maybe she didn't like his apple turnovers. Or maybe she did, but he never made them for her. Maybe he tempted her back by baking a whole tray — "

"*Kristy,*" Claudia said. "Enough about the baker. What else does it say in there?"

"Sorry," I said, stifling a giggle. I looked back at the page. "It doesn't say much else. Just that there was a full moon that night."

"A full moon?" asked Mary Anne. "I wonder if that could mean anything."

"Like what?" asked Stacey.

"I don't know," admitted Mary Anne, looking a little embarrassed. "Never mind. It was just a thought."

"Let's see," said Claudia, checking the list she'd made. "A cow auction. The baker's wife leaves him. And a full moon. What could it add up to?"

"I wonder if the baker's wife left him a

121

note," mused Stacey. "You know, to explain why she ran away?"

"Right," said Jessi. "Like, 'Dear Husband, I cannot possibly eat one more of your disgusting apple turnovers.' "

Everybody cracked up — except for me. I had missed the joke, because I was suddenly thinking, *hard*. "Claudia!" I said. "Where's that copy of Christina's letter? I think I just figured something out."

Claudia stopped giggling immediately and jumped up to find the letter on her desk. She handed it to me, and I looked it over. "This is it!" I said. "I'm sure of it."

"What?" asked Claudia, who was looking at the letter over my shoulder. "I don't see anything new."

"It's not something new," I said. "It's just that I'm thinking about it in a new way. See this perfect circle around the date?" I pointed at the paper. "What if that symbolizes a full moon?"

"Whoa!" said Jessi, jumping up to take a look at the letter. Everybody else clustered around, too.

"I think you're on to something, Kristy," said Stacey.

"Mary Anne's the one who really thought of it," I said. "She figured out that there was something important about the full moon.

And I think there is. Don't you?'' I looked around at my friends.

"Definitely," said Claudia. "But what?"

"What if," said Mal, speaking slowly at first and then gathering steam, "there was going to be a full moon on the night of February fourteenth, the night Christina told Henry to go to their special place? And what if, somehow, the full moon would lead him to the fortune?"

"That's it!" said Dawn. "That *has* to be it."

"But how would the moon do that?" asked Stacey.

"There's only one way to find out," said Claudia, who was leaning over her desk, checking her calendar. "February's full moon is — let's see — two days from now! That's Friday night. All we have to do is stake out the arboretum that night, and I bet anything we'll see what Henry was supposed to have seen."

"Do you really think it'll be that easy?" asked Mal.

"We don't have a thing to lose by trying," I said. "All we have to do is figure out how to sneak out of our houses and into the arboretum on Friday night."

As it turned out, it wasn't easy to figure those things out. We spent most of the next two days talking about it: by phone in the evenings, and at school in the cafeteria.

"Okay," I told my friends, at lunch on Friday. "I think we're all set. You guys are coming to my house for a slumber party, as far as your parents know. Watson and my mom are going out, and Nannie will be busy looking after the little kids. We have permission to go to the movies, anyway. Charlie said he'd drive us wherever we want, and come back in two hours."

"What if it takes longer than that?" asked Claudia.

"He'll wait if he has to," I said. "Now, we should really prepare for a nighttime stakeout. Like, we should all wear — "

Just then, I noticed — guess who? — Cokie Mason hovering nearby, looking almost as if she wanted to join our conversation. "What's up, Cokie?" I asked impatiently.

"Nothing," she said. "Can't a person stand wherever they want anymore? It's a free country, you know."

I rolled my eyes and decided to ignore her. "As I was saying," I went on, "I think we should dress in dark colors, so we can't be seen so easily."

"Great idea," said Claudia. "Also, we'll need provisions if we're going to be standing out in the cold. I'll take care of that."

"And we should bring flashlights," put in Mary Anne.

I noticed that Cokie was still hanging around, looking nosy. But I didn't let it bother me. We had a lot of planning to do, and it was *her* problem if she had nothing better to do than listen to us. Still, it made me a little uneasy to know she was eavesdropping. It would be just like Cokie to mess up our plans. And if we wanted to find that fortune, we couldn't afford to make any mistakes. After all, the full moon only lasts one night.

# CHAPTER 14

"Flashlights?"

"Check."

"Notebooks?"

"Check."

"Provisions?"

"Check and double check. I brought Fig Newtons, Apple Newtons, Cherry Newtons, and, just for a change, Chips Ahoy. Plus some great sourdough pretzels for Stacey and Dawn."

That was Claudia, answering my last question as I ran down the checklist I'd made for our stakeout at the arboretum. Going over it at that moment didn't really make too much sense. If somebody hadn't answered "check" to one of the items, it was too late to do anything about it. Anyway, we'd already gone over the checklist before, back at my house.

Charlie had dropped us off just five minutes earlier, and we were standing in front of the big, wrought-iron gate that led to the house and grounds.

The gate to Squirelot.

As I was saying, there wasn't much point in my going over the checklist, but I was doing it anyway, hoping it would help to calm my nerves. I could tell some of my friends were feeling a little tense, too.

Mary Anne kept glancing around as if she expected the police to show up any second and arrest us all. Jessi and Mal stood close together, as if they'd be safer if they presented a united front. Dawn was playing nervously with her hair, which she was wearing in a long braid.

Only Claudia and Stacey seemed at ease. They were chatting about how much fun they'd had putting together stakeout outfits that were "dark, layered for warmth, yet totally hip," as Claud said. She was wearing black jeans, short black cowboy boots, and a black suede jacket with fringe along the back and arms and silver buttons that looked like those old Indian-head nickels. Stacey was wearing black leggings, black high-top sneakers, and a long, bulky dark green sweater. She had hidden her blonde hair beneath a dark green wool baseball cap.

"*Love* the jacket," Stacey said, fingering the fringe on Claudia's jacket.

"Your hat looks adorable," said Claudia.

"All right, all right," I said. "This is a stake-out, not a fashion show. You both look great. Now, can we get to work?" I checked my watch. "We have less than two hours until Charlie comes back for us." I turned to Jessi. "Why don't you lead the way?" I said. "You know this place like the back of your hand."

Jessi took a deep breath. "Okay," she said. "I guess there's really nothing to be afraid of. Mrs. Goldsmith leaves at six, and nobody else is here at night. There's no chance we'll get caught." She led us through the iron gate (it wasn't locked) and up the driveway. "I think we might as well start with the rose garden," she said, "since we think roses might have something to do with where the fortune is hidden."

Silently, we followed Jessi, heading for the rose garden. Silently, that is, except for a short outburst from Dawn, when she stubbed her toe on a flowerpot. "Ouch!" she yelled. The rest of us turned around and shushed her. "I can't help it," she said, limping a little. "That *hurt*!"

"Okay, we're here," whispered Jessi, turning off her flashlight. "Watch out for the rose bushes. They're prickly. Plus, I don't think Mrs. Goldsmith would appreciate it if we trampled them."

We gathered close together and snapped off our flashlights. "Whoa," whispered Mal. "It sure is dark all of a sudden."

"Where's the moon?" asked Stacey. "I thought the point was that there was supposed to be a full moon."

"It's not up yet," I whispered. "But I bet it will be soon. Christina's letter said ten o'clock, remember? We just have to wait." It was dark, but not pitch-dark. I could still make out my friends' faces, which made me feel less afraid.

Suddenly, I heard a rustling noise, and then a sound like a twig snapping. Both came from the area behind us, near the fountain. "What's that?" I hissed.

"I — I don't know," whispered Dawn. "But to tell you the truth, I've had this strange feeling ever since we got to the rose garden."

"Like somebody's following us?" Jessi asked quietly. "I know. I've had it, too."

"Oh, man!" said Mal. "Who do you think it is?" She sounded scared.

My heart was beating pretty fast, too. But I tried to hide my fear. I didn't want everyone to panic.

"Maybe it's our friends, DT Developers," said Jessi.

I remembered the business card I'd found. "DT Developers?" I said. I'd forgotten that was their name. "I just realized something! Remember Mildred Abbott told me about her cousin who was a contractor? Devon Thomas the fourth? His initials would be DT!"

"So you're saying he could be after the estate?" asked Claudia. "That's perfect. It fits. He could be doing the sabotage — and he might be looking for the fortune, too!"

"Shh!" hissed Stacey. "I just heard another noise." We'd been whispering, but now we quieted down completely.

"I don't hear anything," Mary Anne said after a minute. Just then, somebody sneezed. "Bless you," Mary Anne replied automatically. Then I felt her grab my sleeve. "Kristy! That sneeze. It came from over by the fountain!"

Then there was another sneeze, and another. Mary Anne was right. The sound was coming from the area near the fountain. And the funny thing about those sneezes was that they didn't sound like the kind of sneezes a big, burly developer would make. They sounded more like *my* sneezes. I decided to take a big chance. "Who's there?" I called in my gruffest voice. "You're surrounded. Give yourself up now, and we won't hurt you."

"Kristy, are you nuts?" hissed Claudia.

"Nope," I said with a grin. "I just had a pretty good hunch about who might be following us. And I was right. Check it out!" I pointed toward the fountain, and there, coming toward us out of the darkness, was Cokie Mason.

"Cokie!" everybody said at once.

"What are you doing here?" asked Stacey.

Cokie folded her arms over her chest. "I could ask you the same thing," she responded. "And I think I have more of a right to be here than you do, if you want to know."

"What are you talking about?" I asked. "You just followed us here because you're nosy and always getting into everybody's business."

"You're wrong," said Cokie calmly. "I followed you here because I heard you talking about the hidden fortune, and if you want to call that nosy I guess it is. But here's what you don't know. If you find that fortune, it belongs to me. Or, at least, some of it does. I know all about Christina's letter. My grandmother showed it to me."

"Your grandmother?" I asked, stunned.

"Granny Mildred," said Cokie, with a smug look on her face. "Mrs. Abbott, to you. She's my grandmother on my mother's side. That's how I knew about the rosebushes. After I heard you talking about that letter, I asked Granny to show it to me, and I saw the red roses on it."

I couldn't believe it. How could someone as

nice as Mrs. Abbott be related to *Cokie*?

"So it was you who dug those other holes?" asked Jessi. She sounded as if she were in shock. I think we all were.

But I was still working out the connections, and thinking about what Cokie had said. "You think you know it all," I said, "but you don't. For one thing, those roses are brown, not red."

"Brown?" asked Dawn. "I didn't know that. On the photocopy, they just looked black." She paused. "Brown roses," she mused. Then she gasped. "Brown roses! Like the ones carved into the porch railing. It's a clue. She made those roses brown on purpose. I'm sure of it!" Dawn turned on her flashlight and began to run toward the house, heading for the porch. All of us, including Cokie, took off after her.

"Okay," said Dawn, when we'd arrived at the porch, "everybody aim your flashlights at this wood trim." We did as she'd told us. "See all the flowers and vines?" Dawn asked. "All we have to do is find the roses." We ran the beams of our flashlights over the railings, searching for roses that looked like the ones on Christina's letter.

"Look!" yelled Cokie, suddenly. "Here they are!" She was pointing her flashlight onto one of the posts that held up the part of the porch roof that extended over the stairs.

I glared at her. After all the time we'd spent on this mystery, I hated to see Cokie be the one who found the final clue.

But as it turned out, it *wasn't* the final clue. We clustered around to look at the carved roses Cokie had found, but after we'd examined them closely, and touched them, we couldn't find a thing that told us any more about where the fortune was hidden. "I wonder if we're supposed to dig at the base of this post," said Jessi.

"I sure hope not," I said, pointing my flashlight beam downward. The post stood on a foundation of rock. There was a brief silence as we stared at the roses again.

"What about the moon?" asked Mary Anne. "Wasn't the full moon supposed to have something to do with the secret?"

At that moment, we turned around to see if the moon had risen. It had. It was coming up over the horizon, all fat and golden. And between it and us there was a tree, perfectly outlined against the moon.

And at that moment we just *knew* where the treasure had to be.

"I'll find some shovels," Jessi said, running off with Mal behind her. The rest of us moved slowly, as if we were sleepwalking, toward the tree. Jessi and Mal were back in no time, carrying two shovels each. Four of us began to dig at the base of the tree, as the others held flashlights. (The rising moon was giving off lots of light, but we were digging in the shadow of the tree.) I felt as if I were in a dream. Somehow it wasn't at all surprising when I heard a clank almost as soon as I'd started to shovel. I bent to see what my shovel had hit, and after brushing aside some dirt I lifted out a metal box about the size of my social studies textbook.

Everyone was silent as I sat on the ground to open the box, which was sealed with wax to keep moisture out. My friends and Cokie moved closer and shined their flashlights onto the box. Nobody had spoken since Jessi had said she'd find the shovels. It was as if we were afraid to break some spell.

Here's what we found in the box:

— A locket, which held a picture of a girl who looked so much like me it was spooky.

— A letter to Henry, in which Christina told him that if she had failed in her mission to find him, she hoped he would take solace in the contents of the box. The letter also said that she was carrying all her gold with her, in hopes that they might start a new life. (Cokie let out a disappointed wail when she saw that part of the letter.)

— Last, but certainly not least: the original lease to Squirelot's land, with a note on it which said it was to be inherited by Henry. The note went on to say, "And, in the case of Henry's death, be it known that I, Christina Thomas, bequeath this land to the village of Stoneybrooke, which will always be my heart's true home."

As soon as I saw that note, I knew our work had been worthwhile. We might not have found the fortune, but we had done something almost as wonderful: we had saved the arboretum.

# CHAPTER 15

It was a great party; everyone said so. In fact, it was even written up in the paper the next day! The article mentioned the local celebrities, the delicious catered food, and the beauty of the decorations. But for me, the best part of the evening was a long, quiet talk I had with Mildred Abbott.

I'm getting ahead of myself, though. I'd better go back and explain exactly what happened after we found the box that night.

After the first shock, we all became very, very excited. We took the box to the porch, sat down with it, and looked everything over carefully. In the glow of four flashlight beams, I read through the lease and the letter again and again, as if to reassure myself that the arboretum really was saved.

"Mrs. Goldsmith will be so excited," Jessi said. She made a face. "I hope she's excited enough to forgive us for messing up so badly with Mrs. VanderBellen."

"She'll forgive us. I'm sure of it," said Mary Anne. "I mean, we might have done a few things wrong, but the bottom line is that we found these papers. The arboretum won't have to close, and that's what's most important to Mrs. Goldsmith."

"She's going to have to have a lawyer look over those papers, you know," Cokie-the-wet-blanket put in. "There's no guarantee that they're legal."

I threw Cokie a Look, which she probably couldn't see because all the flashlights were trained on the papers. Why did she have to try to take the excitement out of the moment? I knew she was disappointed about not finding the fortune. So was I, for that matter. But couldn't she see that just finding Christina's box was a big thrill? Finding that lease *had* to mean that the arboretum was saved — lawyer or not.

The only thing I was worried about was that, even with the lease to the land, the arboretum was still going to need more money in order to stay open. But somehow I had a feeling everything would work out. And I knew that my friends and I would do everything we could to help.

The first thing we did the next morning was give the box we'd found, with its contents, to Mrs. Goldsmith. She was incredibly excited, and she wasted no time in getting a lawyer to look over the lease and letter. Within days, we had our answer: the papers were legal. The arboretum — the house *and* the land — belonged to Stoneybrook, forever. Mrs. Goldsmith knew it would still be hard to keep the place running on the tiny budget she had, but she said it made all the difference to know that the land couldn't disappear out from under her.

She immediately started to plan a huge open-house party to celebrate the news. And my friends and I began to work harder than ever on fixing up the arboretum, to get it ready for the public. We organized groups of kids from our school and from the elementary school. There must have been a dozen workers at the arboretum every day for two weeks.

We raked and shoveled and pruned in the garden. We scraped and painted the gazebo and the porch and the sheds. We cleaned and polished every single window in the house, including the huge panes in the greenhouse. This time, there was no sabotage. Everybody pitched in. Even Cokie, although she wasn't much help. We figured out that there probably hadn't been any *real* sabotage, anyway. The developers *had* come around (that's why I'd found their card), and they *had* surveyed the place, but they'd had permission from the town of Stoneybrook to do that. We also found out, much later, that DT Developers stood for Danny and Ted, and that Devon Thomas IV lived all the way out in California. All the other stuff — the tipped-over flowerpots and such — was just coincidence, most likely.

By the time we were done working on it, the arboretum looked fantastic. Mrs. Goldsmith said she had never seen it looking better! On the day of the party, my friends and I came over to help with the final decorating.

Jessi and Mal strung tiny white lights all over the greenhouse, while Stacey and Claudia arranged flowers, including some bright yellow forsythia that Mrs. Goldsmith had picked from the gardens and forced into bloom. Dawn hummed as she polished the woodwork one last time with some lemony oil, and Mary Anne helped Mrs. Goldsmith in the kitchen, setting things up for the caterers. Me? I did a little of everything. I was excited about the party, and too restless to stay in one place for long.

Before I left the house that afternoon, I stood quietly in the empty living room for a moment. I was thinking of Christina, and of what her life at Squirelot must have been like. I could

139

almost imagine lavish, formal dinners, and servants to clean, cook, and draw baths. Then I pictured Christina leaving that life, and all for love. I hadn't let myself think about Christina much since we'd found the box. It was sad knowing that she'd never found Henry. For my own peace of mind, I'd decided that she had probably taken the gold and made herself a new life, away from her horrible brother and his greedy schemes.

We decked ourselves out for the party that night. I actually wore a dress. And you know what? I think I looked pretty decent. Nannie helped me pile my hair up on top of my head, and zipped me into the best dress I have: a black velvet one, in a high-necked old-fashioned style. (My mom bought it for me a while ago, "just in case.") When I looked in the mirror before I left, I noticed that I looked more like Christina than ever.

Watson and my mom had been invited to the party, since Watson is what they call "an influential citizen," so they drove me there, picking up Dawn and Mary Anne on the way. Dawn was wearing a floaty, silky green dress and looking elegant, and Mary Anne had on a lace-collared, flowered dress.

When we arrived at the arboretum, we found Jessi and Mal (both in black skirts and white shirts, since they'd volunteered to help the caterers pass hors d'oeuvres) waiting to greet us. Claudia and Stacey arrived two seconds later, and naturally, they beat out everyone else in the fashion department. Claudia was wearing a tuxedo, with a huge pink rose in her lapel. Stacey was wearing a simple black dress that made her look at least eighteen.

For a while, we just stood in the main hall, gaping at the people who were arriving. Ms. Keane, the mayor, was there, and so were the police chief and the fire chief. In fact, all the local celebrities were on hand. I even saw the guy who announces the weather on Channel Five. Mrs. VanderBellen swept in, pulling off a pair of black gloves that went way up her arms and air-kissing about forty people as she waltzed past them.

I was feeling a little overwhelmed until I saw Mildred Abbott arrive in a plain, but classy, navy-blue dress. She looked so familiar, and so friendly, that I ran to her to say hello. I even smiled at Cokie, who had trailed in behind her. Cokie tossed her head. She was still peeved about the missing gold. But Mildred Abbott took my hand in hers and gave me a warm hello. "I'd like to sit down with you later," she said as she headed into the party. "We haven't spoken since you found Christina's box."

Soon, my friends and I began to relax and

enjoy the party. We ate some of the snacks Jessi and Mal were passing, drank sparkling water (pretending it was champagne), and listened politely to the musicians (a pianist and a flutist) who were playing in one corner of the huge living room. Mostly we just hung out together, talking about Christina's mystery and how much fun we'd had solving it. We also watched Cokie, who was mingling with the other guests. (She was actually following the weatherman around, in hopes of getting his autograph. She's so pathetic.)

After a while, Mildred Abbott came to find me. We headed into the greenhouse, which was quieter and more private, and sat down on a bench to talk. She told me it had meant a lot to her that I was interested in Christina. She also told me she agreed with my theory about what had become of Christina and her gold. And then she gave me something. "I want you to have this," she said, pressing Christina's locket into my hand. "Mrs. Goldsmith turned it over to me, and I want to pass it on to you."

"But — " I began. Mrs. Abbott shushed me.

"I know I should probably give it to Cokie. But you seem to have such a wonderful connection to Christina, not to mention that you resemble her. I want you to have it, and that's final."

I started to thank her, but somehow "thank you" didn't seem like enough. Instead, I gave her a hug. I think it surprised her at first, but then she hugged me back.

"We'd better head back to the party," she said. "The musicians have stopped, and it sounds as if someone's making an announcement."

Sure enough, someone was. It was Mrs. Goldsmith, who stood near the arched doorway with Mrs. VanderBellen beside her. She was announcing to the guests that Mrs. VanderBellen had made a generous endowment to the arboretum, one which would guarantee that it could stay open forever.

At our next BSC meeting, two days later, we talked about how great it was to have most — if not all — of the mystery's loose ends tied up. (Including the mystery of what had gone wrong with Mrs. Dodson's plants. That turned out to be a simple case of overwatering, and after a few days of care by Mrs. Goldsmith, they looked better than ever.)

"I even kind of like it that we don't know exactly what became of Christina," I said.

"So do I," said Dawn. "She could have gone anywhere, and done anything. She sounded like she had a lot of spirit."

"Just like Kristy," said Mary Anne. "I bet

the two of you really are related."

"I'd like to think so," I said.

"You *would*?" asked Stacey.

"Sure," I said. "Why not?"

"Because if you are, that would also mean you're related to Cokie!"

There was a short silence in the room, followed by screeches, giggles, and retching noises.

I groaned. "In that case," I said, "I think I'll give up my claim to the missing fortune. I guess I'll have to make my millions by baby-sitting instead!"

## About the Author

ANN M. MARTIN did *a lot* of baby-sitting when she was growing up in Princeton, New Jersey. She is a former editor of books for children, and was graduated from Smith College.

Ms. Martin lives in New York City with her cats, Mouse and Rosie. She likes ice cream and *I Love Lucy*; and she hates to cook.

Ann Martin's Apple Paperbacks include *Yours Turly, Shirley; Ten Kids, No Pets; With You and Without You; Bummer Summer*; and all the other books in the Baby-sitters Club series.

## THE BABY-SITTERS CLUB

Look for Mystery #20

### MARY ANNE AND THE ZOO MYSTERY

I told Alan and Howie about the emu's escape, recapping Mr. Chester's tale of herding the emu back to its cage. They were pretty impressed.

"I wish the seals had been that exciting," Alan said. "Two o'clock was feeding time, I thought. But by the time I got there, they were already taking their afternoon nap. The attendant said they'd already eaten."

I made a note of his observation in my notebook. "Seals nap soon after eating." Then I turned to Howie. "How'd it go with the bears?"

"The bears?" Howie blinked at me for a second. "Oh, right. The bears. Um, they mostly lounged around on tree branches, napping."

"All afternoon?" I asked.

"Pretty much." Howie grinned crookedly. "Nice life those bears have. Eat and then loaf around in your big fur coat."

"Boring," Alan said.

I checked my notebook entry. There was a full page on the emu, and only two measly sentences on the seals and bears. "Wasn't there anything else you observed about your animals?" I asked them.

Howie scratched his head. "I didn't notice anything else about the bears but I did notice something strange outside the bear cage. A weird couple in matching sweatsuits and lugging a lot of camera equipment were walking around. They'd stop at a cage and talk a lot, then make notes on a pad. But here's the weird part — they never took any pictures."

"They could have just been visitors to the zoo," I said. "I mean, lots of people carry cameras."

Howie shook his head. "These guys didn't seem like normal tourist types. I mean, they weren't enjoying looking at the animals. I didn't see them smile once. But they sure talked a lot about each animal."

Claudia, Logan, and I took the bus home. On the way back, the image of a couple in sweatsuits with cameras and notepads kept running through my head. I wondered if they had had anything to do with Edith's escape. Could they be on a mission to steal emus? Hmm . . .

**Read all the books
about Kristy
in the Baby-sitters Club series
by Ann M. Martin**